Ratting
on Russo

Alan Venable

One Monkey Books
San Francisco

One Monkey Books
156 Diamond Street
San Francisco, CA 94114
OneMonkeyBooks.com

Publisher@OneMonkeyBooks.com

This is a work of fiction. Apart from public historical figures like General Douglas MacArthur, Marlon Brando, Porky Chadwick, Dusty, Marjory Kaplan Esq., and Peter di Bono, all names, characters, events and incidents are used in a fictitious manner. Any resemblance to actual persons, living or dead, is purely coincidental.

ISBN 978-0-9777082-5-3

For Gail. And in memory of Mary Fessenden, an extraordinary teacher, friend, and woman of action.

1

We were out in the schoolyard when a pale-blue car stopped on Ivy Street and its duck-tailed driver leaned out and whistled.

"It's Jimmy!" said someone in the row of girls perched on the rails by the garbage lift, knees sticking out at the boys. Veronica Hilly, the tallest and most "grown up," closed her little makeup thing, slid off and ran out through our midst.

Fat John Crocker covered his eyes as she passed, saying under his breath, "Jeez, Hilly, don't bust a girdle!" and spun the football at Arthur Pollock, nailing him neat in the crotch. It was one of those new mini-footballs, about the size of a hand grenade—hard at the points. Teddy Bing had brought it to celebrate our first day as the highest grade at Liberty School, our last big year before the great doors of Peabody High School would close us in, to be rolled down the stair-wells in barrels.

I don't think it hurt that much, but to be funny Artie grabbed himself and danced round, and the other guys started aping it up and that's when I opened my big mouth.

"Right in the teeny," I said.

This is what happens: try to join in and they dive on you like a pack of Messerschmitts out of the sky. All of a sudden, all of them, all over me about what I meant by "teeny." That's what you get when your parents teach you a stupid word like that for your thingy, like when you're four years old in the tub and it pokes its little helmet up through the suds and when you ask why it does that, your mom says something like, "Oh, little soldiers just like to salute." (I always thought of it more like a deep-sea diver popping up for air.)

Wesley Snyder led the attack. Whenever he opens his trap, it's to try and impress Teddy Bing, because "Weasel Wes" Snyder is always looking to score a few points for Bing, who's the most popular boy in our class, by far. Not only is Teddy the tallest and handsomest, but he's also the best at sports. Also his parents are young, his mom is pretty and his dad still wears his army crewcut from being a drill sergeant during the war (Teddy brags about his being a foreman now at the Jones & Laughlin mill). All Teddy needed to do was bat his eyes at a on the rail and she'd keel off onto the cement.

That's why the Weasel turned on me and said, "Did you say 'teeny'?"

Then Bing said, "'Teeny'? What's *that* supposed to mean?"

I squirmed and said, "You know."

"No, tell us," Wesley insisted.

"His you-know-what," I mumbled.

By now all ears were out like bats', and a goofy titter swept down the rail. Then Crocker opened his big fat mouth and said, "Did Martin just say 'teeny'? What's wrong with 'weeny'?" which brought on a shower of shrieks. Then Artie got huffy at me and said, "It's not any smaller than yours."

"Hey, Pollock, how do *you* know?" fat, red-headed Crocker shot back, always feeding the fire. "Though apparently," he added, "Marty's been checking the rest a' yinz out."

Which wasn't true. I hadn't been checking *anyone* out. How could I even?

But someone picked *that* up and said, "Yeah, Marty, how do *you* know whose is bigger?"

"I don't," I said. "How could I?"

"Weeny Marty." Snyder winked at Bing.

"Cut it out," I said.

"Spin and Marty, weeny Marty, Marty teeny, who cares?" said Crocker. "Say, how 'bout it, guys, martinis?!"

So they all pretended getting drunk. By that time everyone was laughing at me, except Veronica who'd gone out to kid around with "Jimmy" by the car. But instead of bursting out like a baby, I just muttered "Jerks!" and stalked out of sight, which took me around the corner to the front of the school on Elmer Street. But there was Miss Giltenbooth staring out from the principal's office, so I cut across Elmer and ran up the alley to Walnut to kill the rest of lunch.

And this is where I get to the whole point of this story which is: Don't make friends with the new kid. The best thing you can do at the start of eighth grade, if a new kid is there, is to get the teasing turned on him instead of you this year.

Anyway, there I was on Walnut so I crossed to look at the "now-playing" posters in the windows of the Shadyside. The last thing I'd seen there (on Arthur's evening birthday outing) had been "The House of Wax" which had given me nightmares for weeks. Now it was showing "Peyton Place"—not a movie for kids—in a double feature with a re-run, "Come Back, Little Sheba," which also wasn't meant for kids. When

I crossed back over, he was outside the grocery scarfing a box of powdered donuts and guzzling a quart of milk. I shouldn't have let myself even notice him sitting there by himself on the curb. I wouldn't even have known his name except Mrs. Heiler had made him introduce himself that morning. It wasn't his face I recognized so much as his goofy shirt. It had up-and-down black-and-yellow stripes, like a rider might wear in a horse race. The other thing we'd all noticed about this new guy, Arnold Russo, was he looked older than anyone else. He wasn't necessarily taller, but still there was something that looked older, especially with his sleeves rolled up. His hair was dark and might have been curly if it hadn't been barbered that short. His face wore a deep summer tan that never would completely fade. He grinned and waved the donuts at me; for half a second I almost grinned back, almost reached for one but caught myself and headed back toward school.

That afternoon Mrs. Heiler was passing out paper when someone belched from the back of the room. I glanced back at Arnold Russo, remembering how he'd chugged that whole bottle of milk. A couple kids giggled and Mrs. Heiler turned and for the first time made that icy face we'd heard so much about. We'd been told to expect it a lot, since she'd been teaching eighth grade ever since the Civil War, so long that her short silver hair had shellacked itself into a helmet. But she couldn't be sure where the belch had come from, so she let it pass and ordered, "One sheet apiece. Everyone should have a pencil."

Of course I was ready as always with my own two pencils, laid out in the slots at the top of my desk: two new Ticonderogas. And everyone else looked ready to go except the new kid, Russo, who held up his hand like he needed to borrow. Mrs. Heiler stared at him a sec, then asked if someone had an extra they could lend, and then caught sight of mine, looked down at her chart and back at me and said, "Martin Badger? 'Marty'? Is that what you're called?"

Fat Crocker flashed a grin like he just might suggest some other things I could be called, and other grins peaked out around him. To shut that off quick I said, "Either's okay," and handed a pencil back to Russo. It didn't mean we were married.

Then Mrs. Heiler ordered us to each write down any adverbs we could think of while she took a moment out of the room. Of course, as soon as she left, the whole class started talking. Right off, I could hear Arnold asking Veronica, sitting next to him, what was an adverb. His asking her was strange because, for one thing, Veronica was the last one in the room, besides him, to know what adverbs were, but also because none of us guys hardly said anything to her now because of how she'd grown the last year and it wasn't only taller. The other way she'd "grown" made it hard for us to look at her without looking places besides her face. Did I mention her last name was Hilly? The name already fit her so well that, once and only once, last spring, Artie Pollock had got up the nerve to sing that Fats Domino song "I Found My Thrill on Blueberry Hill"—only changing it to

I found my thrills
On Veronica's hills....

5

That's as far as he got before she knocked him down. Whenever she caught me glancing her way, I could almost taste that smack.

Russo was telling her my pencil was a number 3 Ticonderoga and showing her the number. "That's a very good pencil," he said.

A very good pencil? *Shut up!* was all I could think because—well, as you may or may not know—and it's surprising how many people don't— what the number on a pencil tells you is how hard the lead is. For example, a number 1 pencil is what they use in first grade because it writes like fudge and six-year-olds don't care how much it smears. A number 2 doesn't smudge as much, but the point still wears down fast. The number 3 holds its point but still makes a dark enough line: that's why I choose number 3's. I'm sorry to bore you with all these details, but it bugged me to hear this Arnold Russo going on about how swell I was for lending him something. I mean, it was still just a pencil.

Then Snyder the Weasel looked around and said, "Gosh, is that really a number 3? Gee whiz!"

Then Crocker held up his pencil and said, "Hmm, mine's a number 26," and right at that moment Mrs. Heiler came back in the room (she must have been listening from out in the hall) and squeakily wrote on the board:

> *Our class will maintain a courteous silence when*
> *Mrs. Heiler is out of the room.*

"One hundred times, tonight," she announced as she put down the chalk.

Someone groaned.

"Let's make that a hundred and fifty," she said.

After school, fat Crocker renamed her *Mrs. Hitler*, and that's what everyone called her after that. But somehow the blame for the punishment ended up on me. The last thing I heard as I unlocked my bike was Arthur whining, "See what you did, Marteeny?"

I hope you see what I mean about new kids. Take my advice.

And we're not even done with the pencils. That night at supper Dad was talking about the Nash Rambler, the '57, he wanted to buy at the end of the year when the dealers knocked down their prices to make room for the new '58s. Ever since I was little we'd driven a Kaiser Traveler.

I said, "Know what car I saw today, Dad?" I meant the one that had pulled up at lunchtime, that Veronica had run out to the guy.

"No, what?" said Pammy who, still being ten, had no idea that cars are different.

"Never mind," I told her.

"What?" said Mom, who didn't care much either, but was taking Pamela's side.

"A '50 Stoodie," I said. "Aero blue."

"Arrows aren't blue," said Pam.

"*Aero*, not arrow," I said. "Like in 'aeroplane.'"

"Well, peachy," said Pam.

"Sweetheart, don't be snide," said Mom.

"Yeah, that 1950 Studebaker Champion," Dad said wisely. "I think I know what you mean."

Pam said, "Candy's parents just bought a convertible." Candy was Pammy's fifth-grade friend and Teddy Bing's cute little sister.

"What make?" I asked as a challenge.

"I said convertible," she said.

"That's not a make," I informed her. "It's a Chevrolet Impala, and it looks like a tub."

"A tub?" said Mom.

"Yeah, not just because the top goes down but because the Impala's so square all around and the tailfins lay out flat like broken bunny ears. It's stupid."

"*Lie*," said Mom, "the tailfins *lie*. And nothing is *stupid*."

"Okay, it's still an ugly car."

In fact, since Teddy's dad had bought it last spring, it was everyone's favorite car at school. I mean everyone's but mine. But about the Stoodie what I meant— why I liked it—was it had the greatest look. For one thing, the windshield looked like the cockpit glass off the Mustang, the U.S. fighter from World War II, or like the English Spitfire that had won the Battle of Britain. The whole car had the look of one of those old fighters, with its bullet-nose front so that if you stuck on a propeller and wings, you could probably fly it around. But Dad knew that—he'd been an officer on the *U.S.S. Missouri*. And I knew it, too, so there wasn't any need to say it.

"By the way, how was school?" said Mom.

"Peachy," said Pam, but this time she meant it.

"Yeah, peachy," I said, too.

My parents knitted their brows.

"Already, again?" said Dad.

My mother looked at me like some poor, pathetic orphan and said, "Would you like to talk about it?"

I said no, I wouldn't, but then to not be rude I told about it anyway—not the part about teenies or weenies, but the part about the pencil.

"Doesn't anyone want to know about *my* day?"

asked Pam.

"In a moment, dear," said our mother, turning back to me. "That was a nice thing to do—to let him have a pencil."

"Mom, you don't know this kid," I said.

"But he's new, you said, so neither do you. Where's he from?"

"The Black Lagoon."

"What makes you think the two of you won't get along?"

"I know if they see him and me together, I won't have any friends." Not that I had any real friends now.

"Don't be silly," she said. "Anyway, I fail to see what terrible thing has happened on your first day back. Unless there's more."

"Won't anyone listen to *me*?" said Pam.

"No," I said.

"In a minute, precious," said Dad and turned back on me. "Any other new boys in your class?"

"No."

"New girls?" asked Mom and named a few of the old ones. I tuned out the list because the guys in my class had used up most of the girls by the end of seventh grade, all except Veronica and one or two others who wore the most makeup and ran around with high school boys or maybe even older.

Then Dad starts talking about Mr. Greenbaum who worked with him downtown at the headquarters of Pittsburgh Plate Glass. The Greenbaums lived on Chatham Road, which winds up into Squirrel Hill a couple blocks from our house. A lot of times, Mr. Greenbaum drove Dad to work so Mom could keep the car. You'd never forget Mr. Greenbaum's car. It's French. It's called a Citroën (don't ask me what those two dots mean!), which is how the French say lemon. And that's what it looks like, too—a big, gray lemon, squashed. It's weird: when the motor is off, the car sinks down like a frog on its haunches. That's because the suspension works on air. Every time you start that car, you have to wait until the engine pumps up some tubes enough with air to raise the body of the car. What's stupider than that?

Dad said something about how the oldest Greenbaum kid, a kid named Nick, was starting sixth or seventh grade at Allderdice, the junior-senior high school off on the other side of Squirrel Hill. Dad added something about how maybe Nick and Pammy should meet—a funny idea that he thought Pammy at her age would have anything to do with boys.

I said, "Peachy,"

Mom shot me a glance meaning, *Don't you be snide, either, young man.*

That evening I was supposed to start up music lessons again, but I hadn't practiced much all summer, and wasn't too eager to go. Dad said okay, I could start next week, if that was all right with Mr. Marjavi.

We were still at table when the doorbell rang. Mom thought it was the paper boy collecting, so she had me get some quarters from the jar. When I opened the front door, there was Arnold Russo in that black and yellow shirt. He saw the napkin in my belt and said. "You eatin'?"

What does it look like? I wanted to say, but before I could say it he held out my pencil.

"Here ya go," he said.

"Keep it," I said, "it's yours."

"No, no, it's yours." He peered in over my shoulder, sniffed our supper, standing there until I said, "I mean it, you can keep the pencil."

"No, no," he backed away. "I always pay things back." He looked along the porch. "That your bike? Mind my lookin' 'er over?"

"I guess not," I said, but followed him out. "It's a Raleigh Roadster," I added, in case he didn't notice.

He squatted to look at the three-speed hub. "Go on and finish eatin'," he said.

It was chained to the railing, so I guessed he couldn't steal it.

"That was Arnold Russo," I said, laying the pencil beside my plate.

"He brought it back?" Mom looked impressed.

"Quiet," I said, "he's still outside."

"He came all the way here to drop off a pencil?" Dad asked.

My sentiments exactly.

Mom gave Dad a look and said, "I think he wants to make friends."

"Well, don't look at me," I said.

"We could ask him in for dessert," she said.

"Oh no, we don't."

"Go ask him in."

"Mom!"

"Go on. Be nice."

"Okay, sure."

But I stalled a couple minutes more, and when I finally went back he was gone. Then I noticed under the edge of the doormat, a little chit, the tear-off receipt that the paper boy gives you when you pay. That was weird. I took it in and handed it over, saying

11

how he must have come while Russo was still hanging on the porch, and Russo must have paid him.

"Really?" said Mom. "How strange."

"See?" I said. "He's weird."

After supper I called Mr. Marjavi and went upstairs to my room and started to number lines on a tablet so I'd know when I'd reached 150 times of *Our class will maintain a courteous silence when Mrs. Heiler is out of the room.* Then I started cramming them in. But on line number one, I wrote *Mrs. Hitler* by mistake and had to throw that sheet away.

Outside in the sycamores, the locusts were singing away. It wasn't much past seven o'clock, the light still gold on the trees. I renumbered lines for page number one, wrote out the first few sentences, got bored, and decided to practice instead. I harnessed up and ran off a couple of scales and a rusty "Tennessee Waltz." Then I gave up on that and went out.

I got out my bike and pedaled west on Kentucky Street, two blocks to Paradise. That's what we called the vacant lot at Kentucky and College. The lot reaches up the length of the block along College Street to Fifth Avenue, which comes all the way out from downtown. Fifth and College is just about where, across the street, the road winds up to Chatham College, which is a college for women. Paradise used to have a big house with a backyard facing Kentucky and the front yard facing Fifth, but now all there was bushes and sumacs and a limestone staircase of five or six steps that used to go up to a small back porch. All summer I'd gone there evenings to sit on those steps, to be alone and think.

I pulled in and sat in my usual step, was sniffing the warm, dingy late-summer air and listening in on the six-legged serenade when someone I couldn't see through the bushes came onto the upper yard. A moment later, a boy about six popped out and ran right up the stairs beside me, hardly batting an eye. From the top he yelled for someone to watch him jump off. It wasn't four feet to the ground, but he seemed to think it was fifty. He yelled, "Hey, you guys, watch!" No answer came back but he jumped off anyway, landed with a grunt, and ran around and up past me again for another daring leap.

"Tommy!" he yelled.

It could have been only the angle I caught of his face, but he looked to me like maybe half Korean or Chinese. I couldn't say for sure because, as far as I knew, I'd never actually seen a half-Oriental kid. I'm not sure there's even any Chinese people in Pittsburgh, but we'd seen a few at Disneyland.

Something got into me then about this little kid's frustration at not getting Tommy's attention, and when he jumped again I decided I'd make the moment a little more exciting, so I said, "Bombs away on Tokyo!" which is what Jimmy Doolittle said when he led the first sneak attack on Tokyo a little after Pearl Harbor. When he landed (not Doolittle—he didn't land his plane, he just parachuted out of it over China after it ran out of fuel—I mean the kid) he (the kid) looked up at me like I'd said something terrific, and from then on every time he jumped he yelled something like "Bombs away!"

"Don't wear it out," I told him after half a dozen leaps. "You've already wiped out the Japs." Of course, I'd never have said that if I'd had known at the time who he was, because when I said *Japs* he got up from the dirt and gave me a look like maybe he was half-Japanese.

"Reggie!" someone shouted from the other side of the bushes. It sounded like an older girl. "Reggie?! Come or else!"

"Rats!" he said, and vanished back up through the bushes toward Fifth, and I stretched out in the peace and quiet and pulled up a timothy stalk to chew. The locusts were on again full blast. Across the yard, a squirrel ran a few feet up a crabapple tree and stopped a moment to consider. I got up for a better look, wondering if a squirrel would actually eat those hard, tiny apples. I'd taken two steps when the squirrel jumped off and bounced out of sight. I went over to the tree and looked up thinking I might try and taste one myself (though everyone said they were bitter). I raised a hand but stopped at the sight of something on the trunk about six inches over my head.

Man, it was ugly!—fat and milky-yellow green, with bug eyes sticking out like turrets on a B-17. I backed away, said, "Whew!" and went in again for another look. This time I saw two heads, one on top of the other. I could have lost my supper looking at it until I realized what it had to be: a locust climbing out of its shell. See, what happens, like Mr. Marjavi told me once, is a locust (but their real name was *cicada*) starts out as a grub in the ground. For seventeen years he stays down there, sucking roots until he turns into a beetle. Then one fall morning, the thing burrows out of the ground, crawls up a tree all day and waits until his back (the back of his shell) splits open and, slowly, the inside part of him climbs out. As it does, some stuff on his back flattens out and dries and turns into wings. Once the locust is all the way out, he fans the wings a while, flies up higher in the trees and starts making a racket until some female locust finds him and they mate and both of them die.

The way Mr. Marjavi had described it—he used to work as a groundsman—it didn't sound like a great life to me, all those years in the ground and then about two days in some treetop screaming bloody murder, but that's what I was seeing now and hearing all around me. This locust was squeezing, slowly, out of a shell that looked way too small for it to ever have been inside, like when a chute pops out of a parachute pack, a mushroom filling the sky.

But this locust, it didn't look like a mushroom—more like a big cigar butt bursting out of a dark yellow cellophane wrapper, and as I watched I noticed that one of its wings was not unfurling and was looking like it might be snagged and never get all the way out. And all around Paradise, the other locusts were screaming at it like if both wings didn't open, that locust was as doomed as a turret ball gunner whose bomber went down and he never got his parachute on.

I backed away and almost fainted when I caught myself and looked again, not sure I wanted to know what became of this poor, ugly bug. What if the only way it could get out of the shell was to chew off the wing that was stuck and try to fly somewhere on one wing? I pictured it twirling out of the sky like a crippled fighter trailing smoke.

It was getting dark by then, and the headlight on my bike was dead and my parents had warned me before about riding at night without lights. Still, I stayed a few more minutes before I headed home. Last I saw, the locust still wasn't loose.

By the way, I still don't think it was ever Russo's fault or mine that Jimmy's Stoodie ended up as messed up as it did. Maybe we made a few mistakes, but there were reasons. I mean, haven't you ever reached a point of feeling stuck forever?

By my box of Shredded Wheat was an envelope with a dollar and a note to his mother.

"Can't we mail it instead?" I asked. "Can't we look up their address in the phone book like he did to me?"

"Give it to him at school," my mother insisted. "By the way, you sounded nice last night."

Pam rolled her eyes.

"What's wrong with the damn accordion?" I said.

Mom glared at me for cursing. Pam smirked. She knew as well as everyone else, what was wrong with the accordion was that no one was playing it anymore, at least as far as I could tell, in Pittsburgh anyway. No one except me and Mr. Marjavi, and Dusty in her cowgirl suit. She played it every night at six forty-five on channel 2, sponsored by the Wilkens EZ Credit Jewelry Company. Of all the Wilkens EZ Credit Ranch Girls, Dusty was my favorite, not just because of what she played but also because of how sad and friendly and lonesome she looked whenever the picture got her up close. Dusty seemed like someone who'd be nice to talk to, if only you could talk to a girl on TV. They sang country style, but the song they sang the most those days was a corny one called "How Much is that Doggy in the Window." At the end of a line now and then, the guitar girl, Sandy, would bark like a puppy. The song was all about wanting to buy a dog for her sweetheart so he wouldn't miss her while she went to California. The dog was meant to cheer him up.

Perry Como on TV had started out as a barber in Pittsburgh, but even he didn't have accordions on his show, not even for Italian songs. And Lawrence Welk was polka. Elvis Presley played guitar. So did the Everly Brothers and Rickey Nelson and everyone under the age of a hundred. Mr. Marjavi said it was sad how all kids did these days was beat guitars.

I biked to school that day and Russo was wearing another shirt with too much color. I saved myself from going blind by not looking back at him that morning and avoiding him at lunch. When school let out at 3:45, out at the lockers, I handed him the envelope, said, "This is from my mom," and grabbed my stuff to go. But before I could scram he opened it, took out the dollar and tried to hand it back.

"It's not from me," I said.

Fat Crocker overheard and said, "What's going on between yinz two? Russo's payin' off Marteeny!"

"Naw," said Russo. "His mom just wants to pay me back."

"Hey, guys," said Crocker. "Marteeny's mother's payin' hush money to Arnold Russo!"

I tried to ignore that. So did Russo. He buried his face in the note.

"Look, take back the stupid dollar," I said.

"Take it, Russo" said Crocker. "Mrs. Badger loves you!"

"Come on, guys," said Teddy, impatient to get us outside on the field so he could practice throwing passes. The others followed him out, leaving me there still with Russo while he took forever reading half a dozen words.

"Take it," I repeated, though I'd begun to think it

wasn't my fault if Russo was giving the dollar to me. I might as well keep it as take it home and get told how I should have made him keep it. I thought about the tiny store on Ellsworth Avenue where a lady called Kate sold newspapers, magazines, milk, and penny candy.

In my mind I was already gnawing on a Turkish Delight when Russo closed the note and said, "I got it. See, your mom, she's the lady of the house, and what she's thinkin' is maybe I paid him for some days the paper boy never delivered. So what's he gonna do next time if he gets paid for papers he never delivered? He's gonna start stealing more of your papers and sellin' 'em off somewhere else. You gotta watch those guys. Anyways, she'll feel insulted if I don't take it back."

So he took the dollar back and followed me out and waited while I got my bike.

"Which way you headed?" he said.

Next thing I knew we were walking out the gate together, which meant I had to walk my bike or else be rude and get on and ride off without him. I felt like the barefoot man in the cartoon with the crab holding onto his toe. From then on, Russo never shut up, telling me all the things a woman had to do as "lady of the house."

We crossed at the corner where Artie stood on Safety Patrol, and Artie said, "Hi, Marteeny, forgot how to ride?"

"Hey, buddy," Russo called.

At every corner I'd say, "I go this way," meaning not with him. At last, after five or six blocks, finally the message seemed to get through. At the next corner he stopped and said, "Well, we both got things to do."

He took a couple steps away and said, "So long, Mar-teeny."

"Don't call me that!" I said.

He looked surprised. "I thought that's what they call you." Then he shrugged and said, "Okay, well, see ya."

I liked my time after school each day. I could spend the rest of the afternoon hanging out watching "The Little Rascals" or doing something else alone. I was finishing a book called *The Bridges at Toko-Ri*. I'd already seen the movie with Mickey Rooney where he played the helicopter pilot rescuing aces who'd got shot down over North Korea.

When I finish a story like that where all the heroes die, I can't help feeling big-hearted myself, so I loosened up next day and let Russo walk me home. He mostly talked about stuff he had to do when he got home. He kept a shopping list in his head (he said it was quicker than writing things down) that always included bell peppers, in case there were some at the store. I wasn't sure what a bell pepper was; it wasn't something my mother thought we'd eat; but Russo said a good one felt waxy without some sneaky grocer waxing it up. Also, when you bought tomatoes, you had to pick the good ones. Not that I ever bought tomatoes. He said most housewives didn't know how to buy food. I was fascinated to learn all the things that housewives don't even know, *ha ha*, but I wondered why he had to shop for groceries, like his mother couldn't do it herself.

We also talked about my Raleigh. I was getting a speedometer for Christmas, and he said he knew the

old man at the bike shop on Shady Avenue, and maybe
he could help my parents get one cheap. Pretty soon he
was riding lazy circles in the street, me trotting on the
sidewalk.   Next afternoon, he went into a drugstore
along the way and came out with Creamsicles for me
and himself. He did that the next day, too, but on the
third day he came out of with one for me and nothing
for himself and said he wasn't hungry, and besides the
sugar was bad for your teeth.

"So eat," he said.

I felt bad about that—not about my teeth but
about me eating with him standing there. I guess he'd
run out of money for now, because after that when he
walked me toward home we took some route that
didn't pass the store. Then, for a few days he was absent from school.

I wondered what was going on. Mom said I should
call him and see if he was sick. If he was, I could take
him the homework so he wouldn't fall behind. My answer was, *You don't get well by doing homework.*

"But he's been so nice to you," she said, like now I
was the new kid and Russo was granting me favors.

"Look, him and me aren't friends," I told her.

"*He and I* aren't friends," she corrected me.

That's how she was around then, always correcting
whatever I'd say. But her biggest nightmare wasn't
stuff like *him and me.* It was me catching the Pittsburgh
accent, like when Crocker or someone else said *yinz*
sometimes when they meant you guys, or when someone was going *out* they'd say *aht* , or if they meant *look*
they might say something more like *wook*. It's not like
everyone in Pittsburgh speaks that way. Dad said it
was just the ones who never got *aht*-side that part of

the state. As far as my mother was concerned, if I really caught it, she'd get them to put me in an iron lung.

"Okay, Mom," I said. "So you're not his friend either."

"Very funny," she said and called the school and got his number. Then she called his place and someone answered saying she was Arnold's sister but their parents didn't live there, didn't even live in Pittsburgh; the sister was in charge. Then the sister put him on for me.

"Hi, still sick?" I asked.

He hemmed and said, "Not really," and said he was glad I'd called.

Next day he was back in school with a note from Bunny, the older sister, saying he'd been sick, which Mrs. Heiler opened and read to herself and lifted her glasses at him, hard. Later in gym, he showed me the blisters on both of his palms. He hadn't been sick— he'd joined a lawn-mowing crew for a few days making all the cash they could before people stopped mowing their lawns until spring. I couldn't believe it.

"You're cutting school to cut grass?" I asked.

No wonder he was behind in school, doing stupid stuff like that. That was when I found out he was almost sixteen. Almost sixteen and still in eighth grade? How many times had he flunked? I asked him. He wouldn't say exactly. The problem was his mom had been divorced a couple times and moved from state to state. At least that must have been the problem in the past. As far as I could tell, the problem now was all the time he spent looking not at the blackboard but leaning over toward Veronica Hilly, whispering how he wanted to see what she was drawing so he could really look at her "hills." The truth is, we were all pretty sure that she was also older than the rest of us, though maybe not as old as Russo. For the last two years she'd hated every subject outside art and home economics. She was always drawing long skinny women in gowns. She lashed out fast if anyone looked at her funny. Like if she thought you were crossing her up, she'd say she'd get her boyfriend Jimmy after you or beat you up herself, like she'd done last spring to Artie. Anyhow, Mrs. Hitler (Heiler) was always telling Russo, "Eyes front, Arnold. Start learning something for a change."

Fat John Crocker was the one who got Russo into his first real trouble in class. One day when she was out in the hall, Crocker bet him a quarter he couldn't squeeze himself into the white metal storage closet at the back of the room. Already Crocker seemed to know that Russo could not resist a dare. Next thing we knew, he'd gone to the closet and jammed himself under the bottom shelf and told Crocker to close the doors for a second enough to prove he was all the way in. But Crocker also turned the handles, latching Russo inside. Fat John was just back in his seat when Mrs. Heiler came back.

She looked at Wesley, who was grinning along with everyone else, and asked him, "Smiling, are we, Mr. Snyder?"

Then she scanned the rest of us, ready to bite off our heads. She ordered me up to the board to diagram a sentence, and sat herself down in Russo's seat. She didn't seem to notice anything strange about the fact that it was empty, but when someone snickered she looked around again and said, "I see we're all in a good mood today. Apparently Friday has come on a Tuesday."

We laughed, which made her more suspicious, since we never laughed at her jokes. The cabinet was by the windows where the sun was heating it up. I could see the heat waves rising off the top. When the bell rang, she stood by the door as we marched out, leaving Russo behind.

Mrs. Hitler (Heiler!) taught history to the seventh graders next, and we got the rest of the story from them. After ten or fifteen minutes, they started hearing someone moan. Mrs. Heiler must have heard it herself, because after a while she opened the closet and let Russo roll out on the floor. He'd been hunched up so long, he could hardly stand up. She said she hoped he was proud of himself and sent him off to the principal's office. Later he told me how Miss Giltenbooth had made him choose between detention and the paddle.

"But she shouldn't have hit me so hard," he complained. "Not on account of a joke."

"Well," I said, "As long as you act like that, that's how everyone will treat you."

He didn't seem to get that his clowning didn't make things easier for someone he wanted to be some kind of friend—which I still wasn't planning to be. We'd come out of school, and even the girls would give me that look that said, *Why's Marty friends with him?*

That afternoon we went to his place, which was Bunny's, too, an apartment in a house on Ellsworth. It had a kitchen, a bathroom, her bedroom, and a living room where Russo slept on the couch and could watch late night TV. Beside the couch was his trunk, and he kept more stuff in the basement. The deal was, whenever Bunny's boyfriend came over, Russo was supposed to vanish. Through her open bedroom door I could see a poofy bedspread and a string of rosaries on the wall. Russo told me not to go in.

He poured me some milk and started stuffing laundry into pillow cases. That's how Russo was: always busy with something and moving around. From there we went out to a laundry-mat a few doors down. As soon as the washers were loaded, we went next door to a little grocery where he picked up milk and some frozen foods to take back and put in the freezer. Then out to the drugstore where Russo reminded the druggist to call him if he wanted something delivered for free (which meant for tips). By then, the clothes went into the dryer and we went back to Bunny's so Russo could sweep up before she got home. For that he put on her ruffled, yellow-flowered apron and waltzed around the kitchen.

Later he opened his trunk and got out a snapshot of his dad.

"That's him in 1941," said Russo. "Same year I was born."

His father looked handsome, with dark wavy hair. He was wearing a sailor's pea-jacket, standing on a dock.

"Merchant Marine," said Russo.

"Where?"

"All over."

"Where's he now?"

"Maryland, somewhere," he said.

From the trunk he hauled out the jacket that was in the photo. "That's what he give me," he said. "This coat."

His mother, meanwhile, lived in New Jersey.

He was disappointed when I left around six, like having me as an audience had made the housework more like fun. He still had to lug the laundry home, fold and iron and stow it away. Also he was late starting supper, so Bunny would yell at him when she got home.

A couple days later after school he came over to my place to size up my accordion. As I was taking it out of its case, he looked around at all my models, asking how much each had cost. Right then I was building the "Mighty Mo," the battleship my dad had served on. Russo sifted through its 240 plastic pieces, trying to figure them out.

He was disappointed my accordion was small—the size that had fit me when I'd started. Mr. Marjavi called it a student model, but Russo called it a "lady's accordion" and got impatient when I stumbled through "Lazy Mary," the Italian song I was learning about a girl who sleeps in the same sheets that the family eats off as a tablecloth for supper. Then Russo tried it on for a while, playing long, slow chords—which is the easiest thing to do—and flopping his ear down to suck in the sound. Pretty soon I got bored with his fooling around. After that he admitted it wasn't so bad, though I should get a bigger one. He did liked its color: red. That was one of the things I *didn't* like about it once I'd learned from Mr. Marjavi that the best accordions are black. Russo asked where he lived and I pointed at the three-car garage across the street.

"Over there?" said Russo.

The Marjavis lived in the apartment above the garage, which used to belong to one of the mansions up along Fifth. Those places all used to have separate garages with apartments for their drivers. Mr. Marjavi had been their chauffeur for a while, and after the mansion got torn down for apartments, they'd let him go on renting the rooms.

At my next lesson, I told Mr. Marjavi about what Russo had said about my accordion being too small. He agreed it might be time for me to move up to a full-size model. "But what matters more, Marty," he said, blowing his purple nose in his hanky, "is something new I want you to work on, which is your left arm. For starters you need to listen better."

I answered, "Well, I know when I hit a wrong note, but you tell me not to stop and fix it."

"That's not what I mean," he said. "Sure, play the right notes, but this is something else."

"Okay."

"See, hitting the right key isn't all there is to making a musical sound," he said. "Take your hands off the keys for a minute and listen."

I lowered my hands.

"To what?" I asked.

"Anything." He pointed out through the screen. A car went past. After that, all I could hear was a locust or three outside in the buckeye, maybe the last of the season, sawing feebly away.

"Like the locusts?" I asked.

He nodded. "How's 'at sahnd?" he said. (Of everyone I knew, the Marjavis probably sounded the most like Pittsburghers.)

"Like locusts?"

"Yeah, but how? Listen."

We listened.

"Wha'cha hear?" he asked.

27

As I listened, the buzzing got a little softer for a minute, then picked up again and almost rattled; so I told him that.

"Good," he said. "Marty, what I want you to work on from now on is something I call *playing from the left arm*."

I need to explain, accordions have two sides to play on, one for each hand, and in between is the bellows, the air. The side for your right hand has keys, the same as on a piano. That's where you play the tune. On the left-hand side are rows of buttons for playing the bass notes and chords. Mine had the standard number of buttons, six rows of twenty each, and if you're any good you push a couple buttons at a time. Of course, I couldn't yet play all the buttons or put them together the way you should. So, when he said "play from the left arm," I guessed he meant all that.

"You mean get better on the bass?" I asked.

"No, I'm not talking abaht what you do with your fingers. What I'm talking abaht is what your whole left arm is doing. What's your left arm do?"

"Well...." I wasn't sure how to answer.

"Your left arm moves the bellows aht and back."

"Oh, yeah. Because the right side of the accordion is strapped to my chest, so my right arm can't pump."

"Right."

At that point he coughed and wiped his nose again and pulled his beautiful, black Giulietti out of her cradle by his chair.

"Listen, I'll play you a scale," he said. What's the simplest scale you know?"

"C. C-major."

"Okay, I'll play you the C-major scale."

So he played and I tried to listen the same way I'd been listening to the locust.

"Wha' cha hear?" he asked.

What I heard was that he and his big Giulietti sounded a whole lot better than I did on my squeaky little ladies' model, but that wasn't he answer he wanted.

"I dunno," I said. "It sounded good."

"Hear what my left arm's doing?" he said. "The bellows—how the air makes each note start firmly and then die away? That's what we call decay. That's what the left arm's causing to happen. Listen. some more."

He played a few bars of a song.

"Hear how the left arm makes each note stand aht by itself, or lead into another? That's all in the left arm. That's the secret no one knows. It's not like your sister's piano where the sound is all abaht your fingers banging on the keys. The accordion, the left arm, that's where the *music* comes from, every note you play. Now play me a scale. Slowly. Play me the C-major scale."

I started the scale.

"Slower!" he said. "Quarter notes. Make each one decay."

I tried but it was hard. I couldn't really feel much at all about what my left arm was doing except pushing and pulling the bellows.

"I can't really feel it," I said.

"There's lots of parts of you you got to learn how to feel," he said.

"Okay, I'll try and put more feelings in it."

"That's not what I said," he replied. "Feel what the left arm's doin', each note," he said, "not just try to play 'with feeling'. Got that?"

29

Um, I didn't really, but I nodded, wishing the lesson was over.

"Work on it," he said. "Work on the scale. And *lento* this time—slowly. Try it again, C major. Listen, I'll tap aht the beat...."

A while later I was packing up to leave when Mr. Marjavi said, if my parents wanted, we could go downtown together to Volkwein's to try out some bigger accordions, see how they fit me and how much they cost. When I passed that on to my parents later, they both looked surprised.

Mom said, "You know, if you were practicing every day like your sister, we might be prepared to think about it at Christmas or maybe your fourteenth birthday."

"But my birthday's not until June," I said.

To which Dad said, "Son, a new accordion—that's several hundred dollars, right? You're sure it's what you want?"

Well, that made me not so sure, but a few days later Russo told me about a classified ad he'd seen in the morning *Post Gazette*. Bunny didn't get the newspaper but their landlady did, and on weekdays it sat outside her door until she got home from work. I'd always been a little confused about classified ad, about why, if the information was secret, someone would put it in the newspaper. This one had said, "Great accordion. Used. $40." Along with that was a telephone number that Russo had copied onto a scrap. I took the number home that night and told my parents and they said okay, go on and make the call.

The man who answered said he'd had it ever since someone had left it in his living room a few years back.

He didn't know how big to call it or how many buttons and keys it had, but they looked like plenty to him.

"Oh, yeah, it's black," he assured me, and it came in a big wood case.

I took down his address and asked him not to sell it before I called back.

"How soon is 'at?" he asked.

I told him as soon as I could.

Once I hung up I was desperate. I asked Dad if we could get it tonight, but he was already in his slippers and reading the paper and didn't want to get up right then and drive over to Aspinwall, which was where the man was living. Aspinwall was a little town just outside the city, across the Allegheny River on the other side of Highland Park Bridge. It was four or five miles way. Tomorrow night was my dancing class and Friday evening was something else, and Saturday Mom was driving Pam to some all-day Brownies event. Dad said Sunday was the soonest we could go.

"It'll be gone by then," I told them. "It's only forty dollars!"

Mom said, "We'll just have to take that chance."

"Take it easy, son," said Dad. "The last I knew, you sounded like you weren't so sure you wanted any more lessons."

"What are you talking about!" I said. "Plus, I'm saving you hundreds!"

Next day at school I told Russo how my parents couldn't get me there in time. He thought it over and said the two of us could go out there Saturday morning ourselves, if the guy would keep his pants on that long. We could get to Aspinwall on bikes. Never mind that Russo, at that moment, didn't have a bike. He'd get hold of one somehow.

I said okay, that sounded good, though inside I was wondering why every time I turned around I was getting in deeper with Russo, which I never meant to do. But he'd already wormed his way this far into my life, and a little further wouldn't kill me. My parents didn't object, as long as Saturday's weather was clear. Dad didn't think five or six miles was all that far on a bike, and they liked the fact that Russo was a little older and more experienced about getting places in his own. They'd give me the forty dollars and we could get to Aspinwall by a route Dad would trace on the map. If I decided to buy it, I could, and later they'd drive me out there again to bring it home in the car.

Late Saturday morning we were out on the sidewalk mounting new lights on my bike when Russo showed up on a bike—a girl's bike with undersized wheels.

"That's pretty small for you, Arnold," said Dad, looked back and forth between my 26-inch-wheel, 3-speed Raleigh and his 1-speed, 24-inch Schwinn. "That front tire's pretty bald."

Russo said he knew but it was the best he could come up so quick. He'd raised the seat as high as he could.

"No big deal," he told me, as we pedaled over to Shady, up to Fifth and out east past Mellon Park. A few blocks further on, we glided down a long downhill and under a railroad bridge, across the trolley tracks at Frankstown Road and onto potholed Washington Boulevard. Past the Silver Lake Drive-In, the potholes bent north. Further on we passed the Big Boy, then under tall Larimer Avenue Bridge that spans the ravine between East Liberty and Homewood, past all the welding shops and truck stops, and as the businesses thinned out, past the State Police on the left and the course where they give you the test for driving, and past the nine-story tower of brick where firemen practice spraying their hoses and dropping babies into nets. From there it was two or three miles of gentle downhill, almost flat, with wooded ridges on either side. For me it was easy, cruising along in high gear. I had to keep slowing down for Russo, what with his having only one gear and his knees riding up to his chest.

Eventually the boulevard dead-ended into the road that fronts the Allegheny River. Behind us now on either side were the bluffs of Highland Park and Brilliant Cutoff where my dad had taken me once to look for fossils in the cliff. We headed left along the river, up a long ramp onto the bridge and across to a shorter ramp that dumped us down in Aspinwall.

The front of the town ran along the river. The back of it was a few blocks behind, to where the hills took over. The man had given us a number address on Allegheny County Road 23, saying it was Aspinwall, but the map didn't show exactly where 23 ran through the town. We rode around a while and finally stopped in at a little store beside a beauty shop and Russo went in to ask the way while I waited outside guarding the bikes. It was one of those days that's nice in the sun but chilly in the shade. Russo came out with directions and two bottles of Squirt and we rode a couple blocks to the field of Aspinwall High School and parked to eat the lunches Mom had packed. The address we wanted, it turned out, wasn't here in the flat part of town. It was more of rural delivery place where the county roads wound up in the hills that were still officially part of the town. The directions he'd got were for us to ride along the back side of town, and head out 23 from there. So we finished eating and that's what we did, except neither road at the back of town was marked with county road signs and we ended up tossing a coin. From there, we started up into the hills, me doing not too bad in low gear for a ways and Russo standing up on the pedals until we got about halfway up where it got too steep, and walked our bikes to the top and coasted down through the woods on the other side and partway up the rise ahead.

I don't know if you've ever been there, so maybe I should tell you Western Pennsylvania is pretty hilly, not only in Pittsburgh but even more so when you get out into Allegheny County. Out there, it's up one hill and down the next. Actually, Dad says there are no hills in Western Pennsylvania, just many, many valleys, *ha ha.* It's all winding up and down ravines and when you get to the woods at the top of one ravine, all you see ahead is the woods on top of the next one. Well, some places there's a yard and a house or a barn and couple acres of field and maybe a chicken or two, though Mom once saw a peacock.

After a while we knew we'd guessed wrong because there still weren't any county road number signs, and none of the houses we passed had numbers anything like the one the man had told us. I was getting tired by then, half chilled, half sweaty from pushing my bike uphill in the sun and coasting down in the shade.

"Let's stop and ask," I shouted ahead at Russo. Three or four houses later, he pulled in at a place where he thought someone might be home.

It took us another hour or so, but at last we got onto road 23, and another twenty minutes brought us to the right address. It was a little place set back from the road, covered in grey asbestos shingles, with a rusty Dodge out front of a small rotten porch. A man opened the screen let us in and showed us what he had for sale. It was in a black, leather-covered case with a plush red lining. The accordion itself was black like he'd said and big (and *heavy*, maybe *too* big), and the leather straps were old and curled but good enough to try it out. But it sounded great—wet and wheezy and rich—and the bass chords hummed against my chest.

I asked the man, "Okay if I pay you now—?" but Russo cut me off.

"It's kinda beat up," he told the man. "The box looks kinda old. How old is this accordion, anyways?"

To that, the man told us how his cousin had got it in Italy during the war, so naturally it had some wear. But the notes all worked, as far as he knew, and what did we think we were going to get for forty bucks?

"We'll give you twenny-five," said Russo.

"Twenny-five?" said the man. "I could pro'lly get a hunderd."

I couldn't believe it! I could see him getting insulted and throwing the both of us out on our ears. But Russo kept on talking, and after a while the man came down to $35, and in the end I gave him my forty and he gave me five in change. That's when I explained again how we'd need to go home and get my folks to come out with the car. The man said he'd forgot about that and wasn't sure how much he'd be around the next few days. So Russo got him to give us some rope and we packed the accordion back in its case and lugged it out to see if maybe we could lash it onto one of our racks. Right away it was clear that Russo's Schwinn had a better rack than mine on the

Raleigh. That was good because if the accordion was big, you know the case was pretty darn bigger and I doubted I could ride all the way home with all that weight piled behind me. Russo said no sweat for him and lashed it on, got on himself and pedaled a circle around the man's car and said we were set to go. I wasn't so sure. He looked pretty wobbly to me.

By now it was something like half-past three and the day was getting colder. Luckily the man had told us how to get back to Aspinwall quicker than we'd come. We coasted carefully down from his place and pushed our way slow up the next rise. After two or three more little rises and falls, Russo began to get the hang of things and picked up some speed on the next downhill. The trouble was, that next downhill was steeper and further down and right at the bottom was the *Mail Pouch Chewing Tobacco* sign on the barn the man had said to turn at. Well, I braked and barely made the turn. Behind me, Russo yelled and skidded sideways out of control. By the time I looked back he was on his head in a ditch with the bicycle ten feet away, its back end wrapped around a tree. He got up cursing his neck and a tear in his pants and limped over to see what was left. The back wheel was cockeyed, the chain was off, but amazingly, the accordion looked okay inside the ruins of its box.

Well, I'll skip how we dragged it all the last quarter mile to town, but we did and I called home and Dad came out, flipped down the backseats of the Kaiser and loaded us up and drove us home where Mom said, "Where in heaven's sake have you been?" and then made a fuss over Russo, making him come in and let her and Pamela Brownie-bandage the scrapes on his leg.

"Anyways, we got it!" I said and tried to show her what we'd got for less than $40, and we'd managed to round up all the pieces of the case. She sniffed and stuck her nose into the velvet insides and said, "This has to go!" Her problem was it smelled like mildew and she didn't want it in the house, not even in the basement long enough for us to nail it back together. But that was okay; I figured I could get another case. Once Russo was all cured, she made him call Bunny to tell her he was safe and was staying for supper with us.

At table, gobbling up her stew (I was too tired to eat), he told her, "You're a great cook, Mrs. Badger," and asked what was in it besides the things he could already name, and said he might try it at home.

"You cook?" she asked, curious.

"Yes, ma'am, I'm a pretty good cook," he said and told us how he diced up the peppers and onions he used in an omelet.

"Well," she said admiringly, "I'd like to get *my* boys to eat bell peppers now and then."

After supper he made a show of wanting to help her with the dishes, but Mom said no, he'd done enough good deeds for one day.

You might think the first thing we did after supper was see whether the accordion still worked, but I was kind of nervous about that since it rattled when I picked it up; to put that off, we hung out watching "Gunsmoke" until Dad came in and offered him a lift on home.

"You got everything, Marty," Russo told me as he got in the Kaiser, his banged-up Schwinn in the back.

I was almost too exhausted to haul myself upstairs to bed, but somehow I was still awake when Dad got back and came up to say again how worried Mom had been.

"This boy Arnold is a little different than your other friends, Marty," he said. "And sometimes maybe—like thinking he could bring that huge box home on the back of a bike—well, he could use some help with judgment."

"I know," I said. "Anyways, he's still my friend," to my surprise I added.

Dad gave me more advice about riding on country roads, then turned off the light and went out. I couldn't sleep. I kept thinking back on that long ride with Russo and his flying off the turn behind me. Dad said he was lucky; it could have been fatal. Still, all in all, it had been an exceptional day out there, cruising down the boulevard with the trailer trucks roaring by, crossing the green Allegheny (Pittsburgh's other river was brown), gliding up and down Aspinwall's quiet streets perfumed with burning leaves, and all the other stuff that had happened out on those crazy county roads, and getting home finally, achy and beat.

Next morning when I came down, Mom had already wrapped up my newly bought accordion in butcher paper and had parked it on the back porch steps.

"I can't have it in the house," she said. "It smells as bad as the case."

"But where else am I gonna play it?" I asked.

"Not in my house, that's for sure."

"How 'bout the basement—?"

"Not there either."

"Then what am I supposed to do?"

"Burn it. Unless you get rid of that smell."

Okay, she was right, it smelled like a barn. Later that morning, after he came back from mass, we took it over to Mr. Marjavi to get his advice about airing it out. I'd just brought it up to their door when Mrs. Marjavi came out, took one whiff and turned me around.

Out in the driveway, Mr. Marjavi sneezed at it and said, "Yinz *bought* this?" Dad admitted we had, and explained my mom's thing about mildew.

"Well, ya' can't get it aht," said Mr. Marjavi, and told us half a dozen fixes people tried and how none of them worked. Once an accordion got like that, there was nothing you could do.

"Nothing?" Dad asked.

"Well, put your own ad in the classified. Or try the pawnshop dahn on Frankstown, try and unload it on them. And next time yinz go looking, you take me along to tell you what you ain't gonna buy."

That night we tried calling the man who'd sold it to me but he said a deal was a deal, and Mom didn't think it was right to run and ad and try and stick some other family with it.

"But we can't just throw away thirty-five dollars!" I protested.

Mom said we already had. So in the end I sold it to Russo, who only offered me twenty dollars since he hadn't been planning on getting one in the first place. I don't mean he paid me the cash right away—he was broke again at the moment, especially on account of needing to fix that broken back wheel—but as soon as we went out raking leaves, he'd start paying install-ments out of his cut. That would be on top of the money I made myself, which would put an end to my being so lazy, just mooching my weekly allowance.

It didn't faze him when Bunny announced he couldn't keep it in *her* house, either, even after he doused it with men's cologne. He didn't mind because she only meant the apartment itself. She didn't care what he did with their space in the basement; she never put things of her own down there. So from then on, that's where it stayed, and that's where Russo practiced.

Bing said it was weird I was hanging out so much with Russo.

One afternoon as the leaves kept falling, we played football at Paradise. We played along the top of the lot where there were only two major obstructions—a tree at either end. Teddy was the best, so he was one captain. Weasel was second-best, so he was the other. Bing's team was tubby Crocker and skinny Artie Pollock. Snyder's team was skinny Snyder, skinny me, and a skinny friend of his called Jerry, whose favorite words were "fuck a duck." (I wouldn't write that, but that's what he said). Also, Wesley hadn't wanted me but he had last choice. So, though he had the helmet, he gave me the job of blocking Crocker.)

It didn't take long for us to be creamed. Bing pretty much waltzed back and forth, one touchdown after another. Then Russo showed up and wanted to play, and all the others looked at me like, *Why'd you tell him we were playing?* Bing could have given us Russo, but no. Even Wesley agreed he'd have to wait in case someone else showed up, so the sides would still be "even."

We were playing tackle, by the way, and weren't going to last much longer. Russo stood on the sideline as Bing kicked off. He aimed at Jerry. Jerry yelled, "Fuck a duck!!"—and ducked—so the ball ended up with me, and I wound up under everybody, with a big purple bruise on my hip that night.

In the huddle Snyder gave us the play. This time Jerry would snap the ball. Instead of trying to block Crocker, I would see if I could trip him, and Jerry would run out past the dogwood tree and catch the ball over the top. It was our best play of the day. I couldn't quite pull off the trip, but Crocker skidded in dog dirt which amounted to the same thing. Snyder's pass was short. It landed in the dogwood branches, from which Jerry plucked it out and scored.

Crocker got up wiping himself and swearing and yelling, "The ball was dead!"

"Dead like hell," said Wesley. "It's not dead unless it hits the ground."

"That's right," I agreed. "It wasn't dead."

"Say, Marteeny," said Crocker, "do I have to break every bone in yer body?"

Finally Bing gave in, saying, "Let the babies have their bottle." So at last we had a touchdown but were still about thirty-five points behind.

"How 'bout I play now?" Russo asked again.

"How 'baht you go to hell, dago," said Crocker.

Bing's bushy brows shot up. Otherwise, I probably never would have registered what Crocker had just said to Russo. There's not much point in listening to him anyway, since all he ever tries to do is get your goat. That had to be the dago part. I didn't know what it meant, but obviously it wasn't a kiss on the cheek.

Russo's zeroed in on Crocker, turned a little red, then let it go, like Crocker hadn't said a peep.

"How 'baht I play for both sides?" he asked.

By that time, Bing was bored with so few guys to work with, so he announced that Russo could play for whichever team was on defense. Our team was kicking off right then, so we would get him first. So Snyder kicked off and Bing returned, prancing like he always does, and Russo laid him out. The thing was, I knew Russo he was strong, but no one knew he could tackle like that. Then he intercepted a pass for us and ran it back for our second TD.

"That doesn't count," said Crocker. "Once Russo intercepted, your team was on offense. That means he's off *your* team and back on *ours*, which means we either get the touchdown or else we get the ball back."

This time we let the babies have their bottles. After arguing about it a while, we got to keep the ball on offense where Russo had caught it, and he went back on defense for Bing. On the next play, Snyder threw me a long one. Russo could have picked it off but let me catch it and run it out for our touchdown number two (or three, depending how you count). That got Bing mad. Russo swore he hadn't cheated, hadn't *let* me catch that pass, but anyone could see. Even my team growled at Russo for killing the game.

We only lasted a few more plays. Then Snyder started quietly asking the other guys up to his house for ping-pong, and one by one they slinked away until only Russo and me were left.

"Dad, what's a dago?" I asked that night.

Dad looked up from the couch, surprised. He collapsed the front section on his lap and said, "Where'd you hear that?"

"Johnny Crocker."

"Who'd he say it to?"

"No one in particular."

"Well, it's not a word I'd use, if I were you. It means Spanish or Italian, but it's like, at the office if I called Bob Schnorr a 'kraut' or you called some colored boy 'black.' Like calling a Japanese a 'Jap.'"

"I thought you called them that yourself."

"Well, that was during the war. We said a lot of things during the war I wouldn't say today. So who was Johnny calling a dago? Arnold?"

I nodded.

"Well, don't you ever call him that."

Russo couldn't care less about playing any more pick-up football with my friends. For us it was money-making time. Next afternoon after school I pedaled home and got the rake and three old sheets and pedaled back to his place. He'd fixed the Schwinn by then and had his own rake ready. We rode out west on Ellsworth to a building on a courtyard where the trees had dumped plenty of leaves. Russo had already worked it out with the guy who managed the apartments—five bucks for raking the court.

The afternoon was cool but pretty soon we were down to our undershirts, we'd worked up such a sweat. More leaves kept falling as we raked. We raked for more than an hour, even poking under the briars to drag out last year's rotten stuff, and gathered three big piles. The manager came out to inspect, wiping an early supper off his lip.

"Where do you want 'em?" Russo asked.

"I don't," he replied. "They're yours to get rid of."

Russo looked surprised. "I thought we could burn 'em."

The man shook his head. "City don't allow that anymore."

"So what can we do?"

The man just shrugged and wiped his mouth again.

"You sure as hell can't leave 'em here," he said and went back in.

"What are we going to do?" I said.

"I dunno," said Russo, scratching his neck. "I wasn't countin' on this. You bundle 'em up. I'll look around."

He rode off on my Raleigh while I raked the piles onto the sheets and tied the corners all together up around the top. I felt like Superman, picking up those giant bundles.

"I got it," said Russo when he returned. We stacked the bundles on the bikes and walked them out to where Ellsworth intersects Aiken. You turn right there and a half block brings you onto Aiken Avenue Bridge, which is flat but passes over the Pennsylvania Railroad. We stopped halfway and looked down at the tracks. Russo waited until no cars were crossing and hoisted a bundle and opened it up. The leaves sailed out all over the tracks and rocks on either side. As I dumped the second bundle, I looked out and saw a short train on its way downtown—a diesel pulling freight. As it came in view, the engineer stuck his head out the side of the cab.

"Watch this!" said Russo.

As it passed beneath, Russo dumped. Most of the leaves billowed out like before but a clump of them went straight down, plastering the engineer's face. Beneath the bridge he let go with his horn and nearly broke our ears as we pedaled madly away.

Except for things I did at home, that was the very first money I'd earned by the sweat of my brow, as Russo liked to say. It made my parents proud—and prouder when I let them know we planned to go on raking after school.

"Just stay in the neighborhood," said Mom.

We did all right a few more times. Most people had places alongside the house where we could dump their leaves instead of hauling them away to get rid of somewhere on the sly. Russo hustled from door to door. He'd run up to one and knock, and when they said no or didn't answer he'd run next door and try again. He got more jobs than I did. I got more blisters. But by the weekend, Shadyside was full of door-to-door leaf-raking crews. We'd just started along one block when three colored kids came up to us.

"This street's reserved," one said.

"I don't see no sign," said Russo.

"Then you blind," the kid said back.

Russo hemmed around a little, sizing them up. Why he bothered, I don't know. It was three against two, and they were bigger and they looked like they could fight.

"It ain't reserved," he growled, but we left.

The last yard we raked was mine, but it was small and Russo wouldn't let us ask for pay. Instead, he stayed for supper again, kidded with Pam, praised my mother's food, and volunteered himself and me to do the dishes.

In case we were planning to go out again, Dad suggested we try Chatham Road because the yards were big up there, but Russo said he'd already been and most of those places were already raked. Drying dishes, he bustled around, asking where things went. That evening we counted our earnings, which came to forty-one dollars. Since the work had been Russo's idea, he took the first five off the top, and the rest we split fifty-fifty. Then he gave me five from his pile as the first installment of the twenty he owed me for the accordion. He asked what I'd do with my twenty-three bucks. I had no idea.

"What'll you do with yours?" I asked.

"Mine goes for Christmas," he said. "I gotta take a lotta presents back to Jersey."

"For who?" I asked.

"Oh, my mom and Little Smitty. . . ."

"Who's that?"

"Kid brother. Half-brother, what I mean."

He showed me a picture from his wallet. Two-year-old Little Smitty wore toddler pants with a bib with an elephant's face. He was blond and didn't look at all like Russo.

"Cute, huh?" he said, but not like that was *his* opinion. "See, my dad was my mom's second husband. Then there was a different creep, and then there was Smitty—Big Smitty he's called—and this is Little Smitty."

That must have been the first time Russo opened up about his family, and none of it sounded too good. A lot of it I couldn't follow, mainly because his mom had had so many husbands and boyfriends in different places, I couldn't keep them straight. All I could do was nod and look sympathetic at the sadder moments of his story. As for my share of the money, I guessed I'd save it for Christmas, too. In the past I'd always gotten away with plastic junk for Pammy and a model or something I'd make for my dad. Last year had been the bootjack I'd made in Manual Arts at school. That's the first project in Manual Arts. A bootjack is a board with a notch at one end that you use to pull your boots off. Dad didn't have boots that he needed to jack, but he claimed he liked it anyway. Mom always wanted earrings, so Dad and I would go out and look, and he would end up paying. That seemed a little childish now, knowing Russo was buying his presents himself, like a sweater for his mom. In any case, that was the end of the leaves.

After school as the autumn went on, I'd add more parts to "Mighty Mo." The glue smelled sweet, and I would sit there breaking its plastic parts off their stems and gazing out through the sycamore branches, listening to the radio and wondering stuff about girls.

Sometimes when I hung around Russo's, he'd being doing a wash for their landlady, Mrs. Sheridan. She lived upstairs and made him call her Sherry. She would let him wash her satin sheets if he was extra careful about it. When I pulled them out of the dryer, I could feel the heat on my face, but when a corner touched the floor, he chewed me out real good. Back home in his kitchen he ironed the sheets while I read a book or did my decimals and fractions.

Sometimes I'd go off to the bathroom, passing by his sister's room. There was lace on her dresser and a photo of a beautiful girl in a pearl necklace. The crumpled top of her dress was down around her shoulders as she gazed off at whatever it was that shone like moonlight on her face. Russo said that was Bunny a few years back. I was amazed that Russo's sister could be such a knockout. The snapshot beside her was her boyfriend, Carl (She and Russo called him "Shrimpy"). On the wall was a loop of glass rosary beads with the little gold cross sticking out.

If Russo wasn't looking, I might tiptoe in. Sometimes her closet was open, or her slip was on the door. If he was out of view, I might inch open her dresser drawer for a peek. I'm not sure what I was looking for, just wondered what was there. I never looked around too long, so Russo wouldn't suspect.

I wasn't going to say this, but I think I should, so the rest I say might make more sense. One day a paperback lay on her nightstand that made my face get hot. It was *Peyton Place*, the dirty book that went with the movie that had played at the Shadyside Theater. Russo was distracted with mopping the kitchen, cussing over his chores, so I took a chance and open it up. When the book began, it was Indian summer in a small town somewhere, only the way the town was described, it was more like a beautiful woman, and something strange was going to happen. Then some kids about my age were walking home after school. That threw me. What were a couple eighth-grade kids doing in a dirty book? I got a little excited and read another page or two, but all I found was people having arguments while the weather turned to autumn.

Then there was Russo behind me saying, "C'mon, I'll show you something better."

It's not that I wanted to read something dirty. All I wanted was a little—you know—information. I mean, adults would kiss and hug and get into bed and "make love," but I couldn't picture what they did. And I seemed to be the only kid my age who didn't already know, which meant I couldn't ask or else I'd get more of that "Marteeny" talk.

Russo flicked on a switch at the head of the basement, and the two of us headed down. About half the cellar was divided into stalls or wooden cages, each maybe four feet wide and twice as long. Russo opened the combination lock on one of the stalls, went in and pulled the chain on a bulb.

"C'mon," he said.

There was a stack of cartons and boxes with the accordion balanced on top. He found a key somewhere, unlocked a suitcase, and took out a bunch of magazines. The one on top was just about musclemen, but the next one down was different. It was a *Playboy* and on the cover was a woman in a lumberjack shirt, and that was all she had on. One foot was up on a stump with sawdust over her toes, and the shirt had slipped off one of her shoulders, and you could see the side of her breast.

Russo handed it over, saying, "Here, find out about the birds n' bees."

I thanked him and opened the cover. First thing was an ad for a bottle of gin, the next a picture of a man in a turtleneck, smoking a pipe. I turned the pages slowly, like I wasn't in any big hurry, and tried to show that I was reading here and there, all the while wondering why it was people always said "the birds and bees." I'd never seen anything on a bird that looked like anything on me, and from what I knew about the business end of a bee, it wasn't meant for making love. Or maybe they did it with their feelers. Russo grabbed the magazine out of my hands, snapped it open near the middle, slapped it back in my lap and said, "Start there."

This was a different woman from the one I'd seen on the cover—blond instead of brunette—and four or five nice color photographs showed her wearing different things. In the first one she had on a riding helmet and a long plaid cowboy shirt with its tails reaching down to her knees. I don't mean her shirt-tails were hanging out because there was nothing for them to hang out of, because her dungarees were draped on a nearby fence. She was leaning back against a post, with a straw in her shiny white smiling teeth, and one of her boobs hanging out.

Apparently I was taking too long because Russo flipped the page. Now the woman was leaning off a horse, and her hair was messed and the shirt was bunched around her waist.

"See?" he said.

What I saw was the first real photographs I'd ever seen of the things that I was seeing. Leaning over like that, the blond woman looked like she might almost fall off the horse. Right then I smoothed my pants, and Russo grabbed his *Playboy* back and hid it back with the rest.

"Yer too young for this," he said and marched me back upstairs.

"What did you do at Arnold's today?" Mom asked at supper.

"Oh, you know," I said. "Reading. Decimals."

"What does Arnold like to read?"

I should have said he read *Life* magazine or *The Saturday Evening Post*, or that I never saw him reading at all, but nothing came to mind.

"Comic books?" suggested Dad.

"Yeah," I nodded. "Like *Little Lulu*. *Superman*. Plus *Classic Comics*," I added to make him sound more mature. "Other stuff like that."

Mom said, "Don't say 'stuff'."

"Why's Marty all red?" asked Pam.

I could have killed her.

51

That night I kept wondering about the pictures. The girls—the women—all looked so pleased and friendly, too. But what about breasts was so special? What made me get all stiff like that for a breast? Humans are mammals, and women had breasts for feeding babies. That made sense and I knew it as well as anyone else. Why would there be whole magazines full of pictures of them? Well, I kind of knew. But where did they find those happy, beautiful women who let their pictures be taken like that? And then there was that beautiful, dreamy portrait in Russo's sister's room. I couldn't put that together with a dirty paperback book like everyone said *Peyton Place* was supposed to be. I went back to her room a couple days later hoping to find out more, but the book was gone.

"Tch! Tch! Wha'cha doin' back there?" called Russo.

Another afternoon Russo took me down to the cellar again to show me what he could play by now, and I gave him his first basic lesson on how the straps should fit and how to find the bass note of C. I also showed him how to play the bass side, alternating bass notes and chords. As a reward, while he went back up to put some water on the stove, he left the magazines out again for me to have another look. This time I opened one called *Sunshine & Health* he said he'd bought at Kate's. Well! They should have called it something else because what was in it was people at nudist camps, not just breasts but completely naked women and men lying around at swimming pools. Four of them, in fact, were playing tennis with nothing on but gym shoes!

Unfortunately, while the cover was color (with

white lines hiding people's privates), the pictures inside were all black-and-white and most of them had been taken from a little too far away, or a little out of focus in the places I wanted to see, but still I could see how some of the women had hair that wasn't growing on their heads. I shouldn't be telling you this, in case you're even younger than I was, but that's how the magazine really was and I'm trying hard not to lie or cover anything up about how me and Russo and how we ended up like we did. Believe me, I'm not proud of anything.

Okay, you might be asking, like Russo asked me later, "What, you never seen your sister naked?"

I had, but that was before when there hadn't been anything to see yet, and even now, from things I over-heard her asking Mom, I guessed that she was still a "little" girl—sure not Veronica Hilly. But in the pic-tures in *Sunshine & Health*, I still felt like I wasn't seeing all there was. That's what I couldn't figure out: Was that all women had down there or was there something more?

It was raining when I left that evening. On my way out, in stepped a woman in a plastic raincoat, shaking out the clear plastic protector she'd been wearing over her hair.

"This rain," she said. "Can you believe it?" Then she looked at me again and said, "You Marty?"

She had on horn-rimmed glasses with bits of dia-monds at the tips. Her chin was pink and shiny and she smelled like smoke.

"I'm Arnold's sister Bunny," she said, "the gal that pays the bills."

"Oh, hi," I said. It took me a minute to recognize her. That's how different she looked from the tinted photo in her room. Beautiful was not what I was thinking anymore she was. But she did look more like Russo.

"Naldy, you got supper goin'?" (that's what she called him—Naldy) she yelled in over my shoulder. "Be good," she said to me, and shuffled past me up the stairs.

After that, Russo's sister and her room were never quite so magic.

Dancing lessons, on top of the ones we had in school? I wouldn't have gone, but Weasel's mom told my mom they needed boys.

"It's nice you and Wesley are friends," Mom said after the call.

"We are?" I asked.

"Well, his mother says so."

"Anyways," I added suspiciously, "why do they need more boys?"

"Don't say *anyways*," she said. "You're catching Pittsburgh talk from Arnold."

"Oh, Mom, he's not from Pittsburgh."

Anyways, what I'd meant to say was I was thinking there must be something wrong with the girls. But it turned out I was wrong. The lessons began one Friday night, and the girls were cool, and only one of them came from Liberty. That was Drynda Feldman. Ever since sixth grade, John Crocker had been chasing her down.

I had to tell Russo about the lessons, but I was glad he didn't come. Maybe the reason was money or else the age of the girls, since he was a couple years older. Plus, he claimed he already knew how to dance. Or maybe he didn't want to come because he was Catholic and the dancing lessons were held in the basement of Third Presbyterian Church. Still, Arthur Pollock was coming and he was Jewish.

"You go," said Russo, like I needed his permission.

It wasn't like dance classes in gym. There, the boys sat on the benches on one side, girls on the other, and when Miss Geesa blew the whistle, the "gentlemen" had to "walk across nicely" and stand in front of a "lady." In other words, *Act polite but first-come, first-served.* But even if you ran across, the girls had time to see you coming and ward you off with a terrified look or an obvious glance toward someone else—usually Teddy. They all had crushes on Bing, no matter how stuck-up they called him with that dreamboat look. If you really did "walk like a gentleman" or if you headed straight for Veronica like Russo always tried, most of the time you didn't get her and ended up with whoever you didn't want most. Running across at the girls was like charging into a nest of machine-guns, but you had to do it. Worst of all was being left over and having to dance with old Miss Geesa, which was like dancing with a tank. She teased whoever got stuck with her and told them, "Better luck next time!"

Our instructor those nights at the church was the new assistant minister, a thin, bald man named Mr. Runette. Wesley, whose family went to the church, said Reverend Runette used to teach at the Arthur Murray dancing studio. Mrs. Runette was also there, to help him demonstrate and manage refreshments. They taught us how to ask a girl to dance and "standards" like the waltz, the Charleston and the cha-cha-cha, plus some jitterbug as a treat near the end of each night. The boys all had to wear jackets and ties, the girls full skirts. Also, no gum.

The two most popular girls were Julie and Janet Waldek, who were twins and went to Ellis School for

Girls. They'd been on TV together in ads for Waldek Chevrolet, which belonged to their father. You'd see them together in the front of one of his cars, while he said something like, "Folks, get a load of this new Chevy Impala, then come on out to Turtle Creek and try her out at Don Waldek Chevrolet." Teddy and Wesley went after the Waldeks, hoping in a couple of years they'd be driving around in twin Corvettes. But to me a Corvette was nothing next to that '50 Stoodie, and the twins seemed snobby and bored. All they said was, "Oh really?" whatever you said. I got on better with a quiet, red-haired girl named Patty Colby. That's the main thing I can say about her—that her hair was red. The second week, she brought a friend named Margaret Hatfield. Wesley knew them both because they lived close by, on Murrayhill Avenue, which is part way up Squirrel Hill. From up there some kids came to Liberty School and others, like Patty and Margaret, went over the other side of Squirrel Hill to Allderdice Junior Senior High School, like the Greenbaums' son. Weasel was also friends with Patty's older brother, Ralph Colby. The two played hockey together in winter on a pond along Chatham Road.

Margaret was way prettier than Patty. For one thing her nose didn't turn up slightly at the end. Her hair was brown, which also suited me better. I'm still not sure what color were her eyes. I'd say hazel but I've never been totally sure what color hazel is. She was quiet and didn't smile a lot, which I think was her way of being sincere. It didn't matter that she wore glasses. She looked nice with them on or off. After that second lesson, I thought about her all week, remembering her plaid, pleated skirt and pale green blouse. I hoped she'd come back, and she did.

The third night of lessons, Crocker pedaled by with Drynda doing the two-step and muttering, "There's Marteeny and Margaret, making beautiful music together."

"What did he mean by that?" asked Margaret.

By what? I almost said, but to steer her away from thinking about "Marteeny" I said how Crocker might be meaning how both of us played music, if that's what the pin on her collar was for. It was a silver violin, and in fact she did play the violin, but when I told her what I played she didn't say anything back. That didn't bother me too much, she wasn't the kind of girl who talks all the time about any old thing. One thing I liked was she cared about friends. When Patty wasn't getting chosen, she'd send me over to ask for the dance. I didn't mind. I liked seeing Margaret smile.

By the fourth week, we were all getting bored with the lessons except the jitterbug and were mainly waiting for the last part of the night when Mr. Runette would lower the lights and just let us dance. By now I was dancing with Margaret most of the time, but I had to take a break now and then when the little soldier acted up.

Toward the end of the six or eight lessons, certain guys would flick off the lights whenever they got the chance. Also, Bing and Wesley were plotting to get the Waldek twins to sneak up in the belfry with them, but Mr. Runette kept an eye out. The last night's lesson, he or his wife was always guarding the lights. The twins were sick that week, so Bing and Wesley were cutting in on everyone else. Then they managed to distract Mr. Runette away from the switches while Mrs. Runette was off in the kitchen. They told him the men's room toilet was broken. As soon as he went to see, the room went dark, with Margaret in my arms.

We stopped and went breathless together. I was frantically plotting a kiss when suddenly she vanished from my arms. When the lights came back, she was whispering with Patty next to the punch. During the last dance, the music died and the room went dark again because someone had gone off and pulled out a fuse. This time I didn't wait. I rammed her glasses but landed her cheek. When she didn't seem too upset by that, I followed her out to the parking lot where Mrs. Colby was picking them up. I knew Margaret wouldn't do anything more in front of Patty's mom, but I opened the backseat door and said I'd see her soon, though I didn't know how or when. I didn't even know her telephone number or the street number of her house, and I didn't want to ask favors of Weasel, who probably knew. I looked in the phone book of course, but the Hatfields didn't show up.

"We gotta have a party," Bing kept saying after that night. He meant the kids of the former dancing class. Then Weasel told us Patty was going to have a dance at her house and gave us her address on Murrayhill. Mom took me downtown and bought me a bright red blazer with a crest. It looked cool with a pink shirt she also bought me, plus a skinny tie. Once I put them on, she couldn't keep herself from pawing me all over.

I didn't tell Russo about the party, but he got wind. Of course, I couldn't just no to his face, but his coming made me nervous. The Friday night of the party, the two of us walked up together. He didn't have a blazer—more like a suit jacket missing the pants. I mean, he was wearing pants, *ha ha*, but they didn't match the jacket. His tie was also weird—a short black satiny jobby with flaps that snapped together, criss-crossed at his neck like a bat.

As I think I said, Patty lived on Murrayhill, a steep, cobbled street up the side of Squirrel Hill, a couple blocks past Chatham Road. Chatham women's college was sandwiched between the road and Murrayhill. Apart from Margaret, who lived two houses up and was helping Patty's mom in the kitchen, we were the first ones there. Patty's dad was setting up the hi-fi, trying to stretch an extension cord from another room. Right away, Russo got down on his hands and knees to help. I told Patty she looked *peachy*—which she did, but not exactly how I would have complimented Margaret. She gave me an innocent, nervous grin, and asked if I'd help her sort the 45's into yes-no-maybe piles. A few minutes later, Bing and some others arrived and were not too pleased to see Russo crawling around.

Patty put on the first Sam Cooke, and one or two couples started to dance. Russo started eating chips, trying to figure out which girls were free. Arthur showed up. Bing and Wesley stood around waiting for the Waldek chicks. John Crocker was, of course, sitting with Drynda, complaining her skirt was too short. Margaret came in and I asked her to dance, and Patty went off to see about drinks.

Other kids I didn't know showed up, and I wondered which among them might be someone Patty liked. When she came back from the kitchen, all the other girls were dancing. Teddy, Wesley, and Russo were standing around.

Finally, Snyder asked Patty to dance. Then Bing cut in. Then Snyder cut back. Then Bing cut back. You could tell they were having more fun cutting in on each other than they were with dancing with Patty. That bugged Margaret. When the record was over, she dragged Patty out. Then one of the Waldeks arrived without the other twin (I still couldn't tell them apart) and Arthur latched onto another girl who'd come along with the Waldek. Then Weasel Snyder came back from the kitchen, leading Margaret out onto the floor.

"Go ask Patty," she whispered to me as they passed.

Had I caught her smiling at Snyder? Still, I would have done my duty except that right, when Patty came back, Russo grabbed her and sailed her away. Margaret was happier after that and danced with me much more than with Wesley or anyone else, and didn't hold herself as stiff as she used to do at the church. Now and then, looking over at Patty, she tickled my neck with her hair.

We did dance with other people, though. We all danced pretty well together, since almost everyone had learned the same steps. Not Russo. His dancing was different. Actually, he was a really good dancer—good enough to make Teddy suddenly get into gear with his Waldek, and the rest of us stopped and moved back. The next thing, Russo was dancing with the other girl from Ellis. Now there was something to watch. On one end of the room was "Bing the King" and his blonde, future Chevy, like a couple on Bandstand. On the other end was Tarzan Arnold and Jungle Jane. Even when he missed her hand and she spun out and knocked over a Coke, we clapped. They both did great stuff with their feet. When it ended, Russo shouted and popped off his "tie."

"Put on something slow," said Crocker.

Russo sat down sweating, next to Pat. "See, that's what you do," he said. Pretty soon he got her up to dance. When she wouldn't dance anymore, he beat the rhythms and sang along and kept her busy with food. When Mrs. Colby came in and called last dance, he and Patty were sitting together, him holding onto her hand. For the last dance the lights went way, way down. I moved as close to Margaret as I could without pressing in too much below, and she wrapped her cheek around mine. At the end of the song, she lent me a peck right at the corner of my lips.

Afterward, standing out there with Margaret on the chilly front porch, just standing together and holding hands, was almost better than the kiss. I offered to walk her home (two houses away), but she was sleeping over at Patty's. Bing and Arthur came out with the Waldek twin and her friend from Ellis. Mrs. Waldek waved up to the girls from the window of a '58 white Chevy Bel-Aire.

Crocker and Drynda passed us coming out. "Hope it's a boy," he whispered as they passed, and she said, "John!"

"Very funny," I muttered back.

Finally Russo emerged, and Margaret and I said good night. Then Russo and me leapt down the steps and took off running down the hill, sailing our jackets behind us.

"Marty, is she great or what?" he ranted. "I mean, is she great?"

"She's peachy," I said, not quite sure he meant

Patty.

"You done something for me, Marty, I am never gonna forget. Man, I'm loaded!" He sounded feverish. He wrapped an arm around my neck and pulled my head down to his chest.

"Now that's a nice girl," he said. "I mean nice. I mean sincerely, truly nice. Truly and sincerely. And the two of 'em is friends, right—her and Margaret? They're friends, we're buddies. . . ."

An empty streetcar trundled by as we made our way across Fifth.

"Don't think it don't cost money," he warned me. "Remember, the guy always pays. That's the way the ball bounces, ya know. But don't worry, we'll get it. We'll get it somehow. That's just how it is." He owed me big, he said again. I don't know, but the way he talked about Patty didn't sound like her. He called her very pretty, for instance, which I didn't think she was. *Pretty*, okay, any girl might be pretty, but *very pretty*, no. Not next to Margaret. He said she had a nice figure too, or would in another few years.

Back at my place we sat on the steps. For November, the air was almost mild. Across the street, a lamp was on in the front room, lighting the back of Mr. Marjavi's old gray head. He'd told me once about playing in restaurants on Polish Hill, along with bass fiddle and violin. Accordion and violin—he'd said they sounded good together, especially Gypsy style. I tried to picture Margaret playing Gypsy violin, but the image was a little fuzzy. Now Mr. Marjavi leaned out of view, maybe talking to his wife. Who worried me was Weasel Wesley—whether he was after Margaret. Wesley played tennis at the college, sneaking onto the courts. Margaret also played tennis and was taking lessons there. Were they seeing each other behind my back?

"We gotta do somethin'," said Russo. "We gotta come up with a plan."

5

My family's phone had two extensions, but the one in the front hall wasn't private enough and my parents wouldn't want me hanging out in their bedroom with Russo. That's why we used the phone at Russo's place instead.

He had girls pretty well figured, is what he said. Patty had already told him her parents didn't let her date yet. He respected that. After all, he said, she was only thirteen, still practically a baby. (What did that make me?!) First he had to let her folks see he was okay. If they did, the next step was they'd let him and me take her and Margaret to a Saturday matinee, an afternoon movie, which shouldn't count as a "date." Meanwhile, someone needed to host another party. I didn't want to have it at my place, and Bunny turned him down about his. The other guys all said no, until Teddy put the squeeze on Crocker.

Fat Crocker said, "I might throw a party, so long as Russo doesn't show up."

Russo took that as a joke. Sure enough, a couple days later, Crocker said he'd have it in a week or two when his parents were out of town, and Russo could come if he paid admission, which was Crocker's joking way of letting Russo come after all if he didn't show off like the last time. But Crocker was only wishful-thinking about his parents being away.

One afternoon, me and Russo were sprawled on Bunny's bed with the phone. This was after I'd suggested writing letters to Patty and Margaret. Russo wasn't great at writing. As I said, he didn't even use grocery lists, his latest reason being that lists got lost. As for writing lovey notes to girls, that, too, was lame because all it did was prove you couldn't spell.

So we were going to call. I noodled around on his accordion while he stared at Patty's telephone number, which he'd copied off her dial. I could see where he'd written one telephone number and crossed it out and written another almost the same with the digits in a different order. He was sure the second number was right. I stopped playing as he dialed, and luckily she answered. He started sounding very humble about how much he'd liked her party. Then he got around to telling her how lots of boys were crazy for her. He kept her on the line a while. Sometimes he was silent, which meant that either she was talking or they were both just holding the phone. Every once in a while, he'd ask in a low voice, "So, what's new?" like the call was starting over.

All of a sudden he asked her where she was right now, at this very second. That sounded cool. I pictured her up in her room with the door closed, lying out in bed like us. Russo lay there listening, scratching his neck. Then he said, "Yeah, Pat, me too," in a lonely tone that made me leave the room. Finally he hung up and came out complaining her mother had made her get off. About the party he said, "She'll go if Margaret goes." But I wasn't ready to make my call. For one thing, I didn't have Margaret's number.

"No sweat, I'll get it from Pat," he said. (No one

else called her Pat.)

This time the phone was picked up by Patty's older brother Ralph, and he was slow to put her back on. But finally he did, and Patty gave us Margaret's number.

I dialed.

"Hello?" said a voice.

"Can I speak to Margaret?" I said.

"This is Margaret."

"Hi, Margaret?"

"Yes?"

"This is Marty."

"Hi," she said.

I'd lined up several things to say, based on Russo's technique, but all of those were gone.

"I was just thinking of calling," I said.

She didn't say anything. Then I was going to say, *That was a cool party, wasn't it?* like Russo had with Patty, but I didn't want to parrot.

"John Crocker's having a party at his house," I said. "I was wondering if you could come."

"Jeez, slow down!" said Russo. He was squeezing random collections of notes out of the accordion.

I covered the phone. "Could you stop noodling around?!" I said.

"Hello?" she said.

"Hi."

"Is something wrong?" she said.

"No, just here with Russo," I said, forgetting Russo had just told Patty he was alone. I was certain Patty and Margaret would compare notes later on what we had said, and every extra word I said was sure to trip us up.

"Was that him playing?" she said.

"Yeah."

"You both play accordion?" she asked, like a disaster beyond belief.

"Well, I'm more advanced," I said.

"I see," she said. "When is it?"

"What?" *When was the accordion what?*

"The party."

"Oh yeah. We're not sure yet."

"Where does he live?"

"You mean Russo?"

"No, I mean John."

"Crocker? On Amberson." I hoped that would impress her parents, it being a street on the snazzier end of Shadyside.

"I'm not sure," she said. "I have to ask."

"When will you know?" I said.

"We need to know when it's going to be. And who's coming."

"Patty's coming," I said.

"Is Arnold coming?"

"I think so," I said. "I'm pretty sure he can make it."

She said nothing.

"I hope you can come," I said.

"I'll see," she said. "I'd like to."

That knocked me over—her saying she wanted to come!

She let another while go by and said, "Well, let us know."

"I will," I said. "Well, bye."

Russo called me hopeless. To counter that, I told him not to forget all the heck he was going to catch from Bunny when she came home and smelled how he'd been playing in her room.

I was on my way to bed that night when Russo called to report that the party was on for Friday after next. But we had to see the girls sooner than that!

"Who called this time of night?" Mom asked as I hung up.

Next afternoon we pedaled out of school like mad up over to the foot of Murrayhill. From there we had to push our bikes up. We stationed ourselves about two blocks above their houses where we figured they'd pass on their way home from Allderdice, and finally they came.

Margaret looked terrific. She and Patty both wore woolen capes and green-and-white wool Allderdice scarves. They looked surprised to see us but they let us pile their books on our bikes, though not her violin, which Margaret carried back and forth to school. In other words, she was in the same grade as me, but already she was part of orchestras and other things that only happen when your eighth grade happens to be part of a junior-senior high school. Me and Russo still went to a school where the toilets were made for six-year-old bums, *ha ha*.

We came to Margaret's house first, and she and I sat on the steps while Russo and Patty continued down to drop off Patty's books. As we sat, a breezy teenage guy came down the block in an Allderdice baseball letterman's jacket, leapt up the steps between us, and as quickly bounced back down to the walk.

"Oh, Ralph," said Margaret, like she was used to childish stuff like that. He walked on—no hello, good-bye, or anything, and kangarooed up the Colby's steps.

"That's Patty's brother?" I asked.

She nodded. He reminded me of Teddy Bing— same kind of handsome though not so blond. He'd knocked the talk out of our heads, so me and Margaret sat there looking at the leaves still clinging to the maples.

"How old is Arnold?" she asked.

"I'm not exactly sure."

That was true. He'd told me "almost sixteen" once, and you can't call that exact. Of course I must have seemed silly, being his friend and not knowing his age, but I suspected Patty's parents wouldn't like the news (I was right). From Margaret's question, I suspected they already had some rough idea. She tilted her head and said the Colbys didn't want their daughter seeing older boys.

"He's not that old," I said.

Russo and Patty came back, but the girls refused to hang around. They said thanks and headed up the Hatfields' steps.

"We'll see ya tomorrow," said Russo as they reached the porch.

"I have orchestra tomorrow," said Margaret.

"And I have club," said Patty.

"Okay, look, we'll call," he said.

We didn't see them again for a few days, but in school I'd doodle Margaret's name and mine together and try to draw her face. I could never picture it clearly. It was more like a Mrs. Potato Head—parts pinned together on a blob. I'd try to imagine her voice but couldn't do that either.

Russo called Pat every day. Me, I figured I shouldn't call Margaret, since I was going to see her at the party, which wasn't far off. I didn't want to pester. Meanwhile, my daydreams kept me busy. The weird thing was my actual night-time sleeping dreams. When you're in love you're supposed to dream of someone, but I never actually dreamt about Margaret. The dreams I was having are not much fun to talk about. Some nights it was like fireworks going off inside my head—zaps and flashes and sudden sharp sounds. *Snap*, *Crackle*, and *Pop* puppets came out of the cereal box one night and together shoved me around. They also bashed around with rakes. I thought I'd wake up drowning in a bowl of Rice Crispies and milk. The milk part of that was close, but by the time I woke it was more of a cakey, sticky stuff on my pajamas that I hoped Mom wouldn't mention when she washed them or changed the sheets. Sorry, I know this is embarrassing, but I'm trying not to lie.

A couple nights before the party, Teddy called and told me, "Some of us think Russo shouldn't be allowed to come."

"Why?" I asked.

"Because he's a loudmouth. And kinda old. And you know Patty's Presbyterian, like Snyder?" he added.

"What's that got to do with it?" I said.

"Well, Russo's Catholic, right?"

"I guess."

"Just tell him not to come," said Weasel in the background.

"Well, Arthur's Jewish," I said. "Would anyone mind about him?"

"We're not talkin' about Arthur," said Bing.

"Why don't you want Russo?" I asked.

"Look," he said, "You'll never make it with Margaret so long as you hang around with Arnold."

"Patty doesn't even like him," Wesley added from nearby.

"I can't tell Russo not to come," I said. "He's the one who got Crocker to throw the party."

"Tough," said Bing. "Let him throw his own."

"Come on, Marty," Wesley whined. "Just tell the yo-yo no."

I was angry. Why call me? Call Russo, if they had problems with him! Or maybe this had something to do with Wesley's moves on Margaret, or maybe that Bing was bored with the Waldeks and their boring Chevrolets, and now he wanted Margaret, too. Maybe this was Bing's way of saying he didn't want me there. Or maybe his way of saying I was one of the gang, so why should I buddy with Russo? Teddy was right that Russo could be a pain in the behind. He could got on my nerves, too, like one afternoon when I sat in his kitchen watching him sweep and he handed the broom to me and said, "You do it," so I got up and started poking the dust out from under a chair.

"Not like that!" He pushed me aside, flung the chairs out from the table and rammed the table against the wall. "There now!"

He pointed to the space he'd cleared. I started sweeping.

"Not like that. Don't pat!" He grabbed the broom again. "Jeez, I gotta teach you how to sweep?"

Nothing I did was right. I told him, "Go on and do it yourself."

Times like that he was a menace. He'd crash around in the apron doing things too fast. Yet other times he'd put the apron on and still be okay. He'd sing up the kitchen while he cooked. Other times, he got edgy from always trying to keep his sister off his back.

It's true he was a loudmouth sometimes and a sucker for a dare. On top of that was money. Russo couldn't stop telling me what an easy life I had on account of my allowance. Christmas was going to cost him over eighty bucks, including the bus to New Jersey. It was like he was the parent and the grownups in his family were kids. In addition to Little Smitty, he had five or six other presents to give. Every week he got crazier dreaming up ways to make money, and touchier too.

I was also worried about how Russo might act at the party. Even at the first party at Patty's, before he even knew, he'd been wrapping his arm around her neck. *But why shouldn't she like him?* I asked myself after Bing had let me go. Russo wasn't Frank Sinatra, maybe, but he wasn't Frankenstein.

Crocker called it a "Sputnik party" in honor of Laika, the dog the Russians had shot into space. But the only thing he'd done to make it in honor of that was hang a silver Christmas ball from the chandelier in the hall. He'd taped four toothpicks to the ball to make it look like Sputnik. The party was in the sun room at the back of the house, with sliding glass doors to a patio hung with Japanese lanterns. Of course, it was too cold for dancing outside.

Every time someone arrived, Mr. and Mrs. Crocker crept out from the living room to say hello until Johnny shoved them back out of the way. All he said to them about me and Russo was, "This here's Arnold, and this, you know, is Marty, his faithful Indian friend."

Finally Patty and Margaret arrived with Wesley who had hitched a ride. The girls were in a giggly mood that they explained by saying Ralph was funny. He'd just got his license, had dropped them off, and was picking them up at ten forty-five.

"So early?" Russo lamented. Patty acted apologetic, but I thought it was crocodile tears.

I liked Margaret's chuckle that evening, and now and then while we danced, she hugged a little closer than before. When she stood aside, her eyes would glow from the light of the lanterns outside. Bing and the rest were there, and other kids I didn't know. Russo and I didn't mix very much, just danced and ate and sat in a corner next to our girls. Once Bing came over, yawned, and beckoned Margaret to dance.

She said, "Don't you need your beauty sleep?"

Teddy staggered like he'd had a heart attack.

"Aww," he said, clutching his chest, and out of pity she got up and danced.

Around ten, we went outside to cool off. A sundial hung on the patio wall, and the four of us went over to see it. A lantern cast just enough light to cast the pointer's shadow on VIII. Nearby was a small stone fountain. In it, a small naked lady of stone propped a jug on her shoulder like she was pouring its contents into the trough.

"She must be cold," I said.

Russo said the way she had her armpit up was like the woman in the roll-on deodorant ad.

"I think she's nice," said Margaret.

Russo walked Patty away in the shadows. We stayed at the statue and shared a kiss or two before she was cold and we had to go in. Russo and Patty were still out there, his arms around her, very still. *That's what he needs,* I thought, and was happy for him, and felt good myself.

At ten forty-five on the dot, Ralph Colby came in jingling his keys. Russo tried to stall, suggesting Ralph hang out, but Ralph wasn't sticking around. You could tell from his face that all these girls were way too young for him.

"One more dance," said Russo, holding onto Patty.

Ralph said he'd wait in the car, and Margaret went to get her coat.

"Thank you. G'night," she told me in the hall.

"G'night," I said.

No kiss. But of course, we'd kissed about twice already, and maybe she thought that should be enough for one night.

Soon Patty followed. When they were gone, we got our coats and said our own goodbyes. It was a good, cold night for walking. At the corner Russo jumped and whacked the stop sign hard enough to make it sound off like a gong. A block or two further on, he ran out in the street and started singing. I told him the men in the white coats were coming, but that didn't scare him. He had to sing.

> *Sin-cere-ly!*
> *Oh, you know*
> *How I love you,*
> *I'd do any-theee-ing for you.*
> *Please say*
> *You'll be mine.*

He didn't sound too bad. If there'd been more of him, he could have been the Moonglows singing on WEEP. Then a light went on in an upper floor window. The window went up and a head stuck out.

"Hey yinz," a deep voice called.

Russo peered up at the head.

"Yeah, you." the voice want on. Hey, you want a future?"

"Sir?"

"I said, you want a future?"

"Yes, sir."

"Well, then, I'd hate you wastin' that voice of yours on a lot of sleeping people. So what I'm gonna do, I'm gonna tell you where my office is dahntahn, and you come dahn tomorrow morning and I'm gonna give you an audition."

"Me?" said Russo. "Audition?"

"Hey, why not?"

"Are you a talent scout?" asked Russo.

"You wanna' come up and see my card?"

"Right now?"

"Look, I'm talkin' baht tomorrow."

"Sure! Where's your office?"

"Dahntahn, corner of Fourth and Forbes. Be there at nine tomorrow morning. In the meantime, get your butts on home to bed."

"I'll be there," said Russo. "Fourth and Forbes?"

"You got it."

The window went down. Russo gave me a shove.

"Hear that?" he said. And that's how it always was with Russo—one moment just walking down some street, next moment a future rock 'n roll star. Then he started to run, and I ran after.

"Tomorrow at nine!" he said, barely panting.

"Tomorrow?" I panted. "Tomorrow's Saturday. You think he's open on Saturday?" (*Pant.*)

"Sure, why not? He's gotta be. All that undiscovered talent? Heck, we can't come on weekdays. We're all in school or out diggin' ditches. Only time to do business (*pant-pant*) is the weekend. Business downtown. You know what I always wanted, Marty? (*Pant.*) What I always wanted—"

"Slow down!" I said.

He settled back to a walk.

"Bein' a singer," he said. "Wanna know my stage name, too?"

"Shoot."

"Johnny Russell. Couple years from now, when you hear it, you'll know that's me. 'Course, I'll be in New York or somewhere, but I'll tell Pat, 'We might forget the rest, but we ain't forgettin' Marty.'"

"And Margaret," I added.

By now he didn't mind so much that Ralph had picked them up so early. Heck, one day he'd make his own kids get home early, too. He figured they'd have about four.

"You know she's not Catholic," I said.

"I know that. What's that matter?"

I was moved. I said, "I know what you mean. You can't not ask someone to marry you just because she's something else. The big thing is you love her."

"True," he agreed. A moment of thought and he added, "Anyways, she can always convert."

Then he remembered how young she was and how they'd need to wait a couple years. It sobered him up to think of himself as the one who would teach her all about life. He began to sound more and more like a man with responsibilities to consider. I wished I could have remembered half of those things to say to Margaret that Russo said about Patty that night, stuff you'd never forget.

We reached his place and sat on the steps. The building was quiet, but Bunny's boyfriend Shrimpy's Ford was parked out front. The apartment looked dark from the street. The only light was in Sherry the landlady's bedroom on the floor above.

"I want to get Pat somethin,'" he said. "Somethin' nice and not too flashy. Small but big."

"Jewelry?" I suggested.

"Yeah."

"Maybe I'll get something for Margaret." I could see her pretty neck waiting for a chain with something silver on the end.

"How much you got?" he asked.

My money from raking had gone in the bank, but I had about eight dollars cash. He warned me not to think cheap. Then Shrimpy came out, so Russo could finally go in and I could run on home before my toes froze solid.

Did I already mention how much it bugged me when Crocker would say how "easy" the EZ Credit Girls must be? I thought about that now as me and Russo headed downtown to Wilkens EZ Credit Jewelry. For the first time, I had a shot at meeting Dusty. We meant to leave at 3:30, right after school, but Russo had some things to do and by the time we got on the 71 it was already past five. On the trolley ride, I asked him what had happened with the talent scout from that other night. Russo said he'd gone next morning even earlier than the man had said, looking for his office at Fourth and Forbes. The problem was, the two streets never cross.

It was rush hour when we found the Wilkens EZ Credit store. As it turned out, Dusty wasn't there, though there was a black-and-white four-foot cardboard stand-up cut-out photo of her just inside the door.

Already the clerks were clearing the diamonds out of the windows and glass displays and moving them back to the vault. There were some inexpensive displays that the clerks didn't bother to empty each night. That's where I saw the silver thunderbird ring (not the sports car—I mean a thunder *bird*.) One salesman brought it out for me while the other stood by the door to cut off other late arrivals.

Russo took his time, but settled on a broken heart. It came in two pieces, cut zigzag down the middle with a separate chain on each half of the heart. The man said it was solid silver plate. You kept one half of the heart yourself and gave the other to the girl. (As a man, you didn't necessarily have to wear it on a necklace.) To read the message you wanted engraved, you had to put the halves together. Russo said it was better than a ring. He'd get her a real one someday; why fool around now with something cheap? Besides, her parents might not let her wear a ring. He thought a while and finally told the man what words he wanted written on the heart. His half (the left half) would say:

> *Pat and...*
> *For...*
> *And...*

And Patty's half (the right half) would say:

> *...Arnold*
> *...ever*
> *...always*

"Sweet," said the clerk.

I still bought the thunderbird ring. Then Russo ordered an ID bracelet for himself, with room for engraving his name on the top and a skinny photo compartment inside. It took us a while to decide all this and for the man to ring it up. Meanwhile, the man at the door disgustedly flicked his cigarette out at the street.

We left Russo's items there for engraving. On our

way back to the streetcar we stopped at an army-navy store. What caught my eye was a mannequin head wearing dark, wire-rimmed sunglasses and a general's hat like General MacArthur. It was smoking a corncob pipe through a hole that someone had drilled in its mouth, like the one MacArthur always clamped between his teeth. Gazing out from behind his dark sunglasses, he seemed to be looking back at the Philippines after the Japanese drove him out and think-ing, *I shall return.* But what I wanted was the scarf around his neck. The sign said genuine parachute silk and six feet long, on sale for a dollar. Russo liked it too, so we went in together and bought each other scarves, and called ourselves even for Christmas.

By the time I got home, Mom was ready to call the police.

"It's almost seven! What were you doing down-town on a school night? For Pete's sake, Marty!" When I told her I'd gone shopping with Russo, she said, "Well, think for yourself now and then."

After supper Dad took me aside.

"Guess Christmas is coming," he noted. "Any bright ideas for mother?"

"Not yet."

"Well, in case a blinding light...." He fished in his pocket and slipped me a ten.

"I don't need it, Dad," I said.

He said, "Keep it. Gifts can get expensive."

I'd told them where we'd gone, although I hadn't told them why. He must have thought I'd gone there looking for cuff links for him or Christmas ear rings for Mom.

Later I smuggled the phone inside the front hall closet to talk things over with Russo. As soon as he picked up, I heard his sister screaming. "I pay the gas! Rent! Food! What does Ma pay, Naldo? Tell me when's the last time she sent me a check?"

"Hello?" said Arnold into the phone.

"Next time you spend my grocery money...!" She drowned him out.

"Hi Arnold," I said.

"Oh, hi. I can't talk now," he said and hung up.

It was no big deal, he told me the next day. Anyways, Sherry the landlady owed him for something, and he'd get Bunny something nice for Christmas. We decided the best way to give the girls their presents was to combine that with a movie. Later, when I told my parents I was taking Margaret to a picture (it was the first time I mentioned her to them), they raised my allowance half a dollar and gave me six dollars for tickets and something to eat. Dad never even mentioned the ten he'd already handed over. I was making a fortune off Margaret.

"They might like 'Sayonara,'" Mom suggested. It was playing downtown, starring Marlon Brando.

"Sigh-yo-nara," Dad sighed. Sometimes he got nostalgic about Japan, his being there after the war. "You know what that means in Japanese?"

I shook my head.

"It means goodbye."

"Uh huh," said Mom. She'd kid him now and then about how many geisha girls he'd met.

"Of course it's a romance," he said. "It might not interest boys too much. But it's also about the U.S. Air Force in Korea. Might have some dogfight scenes."

I said, "Look, Dad, it's not like I'm six years old."

Mom said, "Don't say *look* when there's nothing to

look at. And Marty, you've been saying *Me and someone did something* when what you mean is *Someone and I*."

"Okay, okay."

After seeing Brando as the motorcycle king in "The Wild One," any movie he made was fine with Russo. Patty told him she'd go, but only if Margaret went, too. That was my cue to call Margaret, who asked her folks and they said yes to the matinee. So early Saturday afternoon I met him at the foot of the Murrayhill, both of us wearing our new silk scarves. To fit the theme of the movie, Russo was wearing his pea coat and I had on my Eisenhower jacket that snapped around the waist. It was what I usually wore in winter, and the day was pretty cold.

We picked them up at noon and took the streetcar to the Warner, the big old downtown theatre where "Cinerama" had played. (The Warner had no double features—one movie was all you got, and it cost way more than two at the Shadyside. Between that and drinks and candy, the whole six dollars vanished.) We sat down front. The curtain opened and we gazed up at the wall of light.

Like *The Bridges at Toko-Ri*, "Sayonara" was about the Korean War and two Air Force guys stationed in Japan. One was played by Red Buttons, the first to fall in love. Red was pretty much an ordinary Air Force guy. The second guy was a major, played by Marlon Brando, who tried to talk Red out of marrying a Japanese girl that Red was in love with. (Red almost punched him out for trying.) Brando was a famous Sabre Jet ace who'd shot down seven Soviet MiGs over Korea, but he was also Marlon Brando so he talked more like a boxer. He was going to marry an American girl who reminded me of the Waldek twins, until he met this Japanese woman who happened to be a famous actress (in Japan). The woman hated Americans for killing her family in the Second World War, but after a while she started meeting Brando secretly at Red's. She couldn't marry Brando because of her job and other things, and he didn't think he could marry her because of his American girlfriend and because she was Japanese. Then Red Buttons got married, and him and his Japanese wife killed themselves because the Air Force wouldn't let Red take her home to the States. That was sad. After that, Brando went to his actress and made her marry him after all.

I'll never forget that movie. It was different from *Toko-Ri,* where *all* the good guys wind up dead. At the end of "Sayonara" was this American jet fighter ace running off with a beautiful Japanese girl. The movie title might mean "goodbye," but what Brando was saying at the end was more like, *Nuts to you, you other Americans who think you can stand in my way.* He couldn't care less what anyone thought except himself and her, not even his father, who happened to be a general. That's what you had to like about Marlon Brando: he was always himself. Somehow it reminded me of Mr. Marjavi and his strange idea about your left arm and how good things come from parts of you that you might not even know are there until you find them.

During the movie Russo tried to fool around, but Margaret and I watched it all the way through, only now and then holding hands. It didn't seem right to mess around when Brando was being such a gentleman up on the screen. I remember Margaret's sigh when he finally told his old white American girlfriend he was set on marrying someone else.

The day was late when the movie let out. Russo pulled me aside and said get lost while he took Patty down the block to Wilkens EZ Credit so he could pick up his ID bracelet and the heart, now that they'd been engraved, and give her half of the heart before we hopped the streetcar home. Margaret was okay with that, as long as no one wandered too far. So we window-shopped a bit. It was cold, and Margaret looked so pretty in the fur around the hood. The lights of the store windows patched her with color. We held hands, walking past a White Castle diner where I would have invited her in for cocoa except she wasn't willing to go inside and maybe lose track of our friends.

All afternoon, the thunderbird ring had sat there in the pocket of my pants beneath my hankie. When and how was I going to take it out and give it to her? Here on the sidewalk downtown wasn't right. Then Russo and Patty came out of the jeweler, heading back our way. He swung her hand and grinned while she looked straight ahead, grinning also in a nervous, tenser sort of way. When they reached us, she and Margaret looked at each other like x-rays passing back and forth.

For the long ride back to Shadyside, Russo settled Patty in the seat a couple rows in front of us. Pretty soon he started a game of trying to put her chain around her neck until she finally put it on herself. After that, all we could see going one was his arm around her neck and him whispering in her ear.

I couldn't think what to say to Margaret, gazing out at the run-down houses that line the Hill District blocks along Fifth. Not that anyone needed to talk except that there was still the ring. What was wrong with me? Why couldn't I just pull it out, tell her to take off her glove, and slide it on her finger? *Which finger?* I wondered, at the same time thinking of what Red Buttons had said to Marlon Brando, long before Brando could understand. He'd said, "Sure, I'm crazy, Major—crazy in love!"

I understood that now. And I knew I should have been entertaining Margaret like Russo was doing with Patty, but what do you whisper at times like that? The whole way home and not one thing except when Margaret said she'd liked Brando better in "Teahouse of the August Moon." She claimed he'd played a funny Japanese in that one, but I thought she must be wrong because Brando would never be anyone's clown and I just couldn't picture him pretending to look Japanese (it turns out she was right). Apart from that, everything I thought of saying sounded corny and fake, even if it was true. Once we got off at Negley Avenue and were walking up that long steep block of Murrayhill, my hand was tied up holding hers. I couldn't make myself let go to reach in my pocket and take out the ring. Leaving Russo and Patty behind at the foot of the Colbys' steps, I only knew it was now or never at the moment we stopped at Margaret's.

"By the way," I said as she let go my hand and started up by herself.

What I'd meant to add after that was, *Margaret, if only I could tell you what it is about you, if only I knew what it is....* Or, *Margaret, you might be wondering why I got you a thunderbird ring, when some people don't even know what a thunderbird is, but....* But she was already two steps up, and all I could do was tear off my glove and send my hanky flying as I finally pulled it out and grabbed her trailing hand before it disappeared. She stopped and looked down in amazement as I pressed it into her glove.

"It's a ring," I said.

She opened her palm and stared and when she got her breath back said, "It's nice," and came back down. "It's very sweet," she said, and glanced around and pecked me on the cheek. Then we looked up at her mother who had just come out on the porch.

"We're back," said Margaret.

"Hi, Mrs. Hatfield," I said.

Her mother smiled. "Good," she said, and "Marty, would you care to come in?"

"No, thanks," I said. "My folks are expecting me home."

Mrs. Hatfield nodded nicely.

"Thank you for a wonderful afternoon," said Margaret, the ring now wrapped in her glove.

When they disappeared inside, I looked back down toward Patty's and saw Russo coming down the steps.

"Well?" he said.

"She took it!"

My bike went down in the basement for winter as a freezing November rain set in. After school Russo was home calling Patty, which bothered Bunny a lot. She was a secretary downtown. She'd call to tell him something she wanted done before she got home, but the line was always busy. She'd just got rid of Shrimpy, so she yelled at Russo more than before. Russo went out and rescued an overstuffed chair from the rain and dragged it down in the basement. Once it dried, he'd sit down there and keep out of his sister's way. Maybe it was spending all that time down there alone that made him start to feel like Red in "Sayonara," living in a secret house in Tokyo with his secret Japanese wife

and telling the Air Force they could go blow if they
tried to make him give her up. In the beginning, Red
had even told off Marlon. Finally Red told his sweetheart, "That's it, Mrs. Kelly, just you and me." That
was before they killed themselves. That's how Russo
would talk about Patty: "Just me and her—that's it."

But her parents didn't like him to call, and Patty
was always busy, she said, and didn't want him coming
over and hanging around. Also, what with the rain
most days, he couldn't get there fast enough after
school to catch her where she and Margaret got off the
bus. And Russo was the kind of guy who didn't like to
sit around. At school, he opened and closed the lid of
his desk more times every day than the whole class did
in a week. Plus he was always scratching. Maybe it
was fleas from Sherry's old toy poodle, Edith, that he
had to take out every night so she could widdle or
worse on the sidewalk. Edith wouldn't walk very far.
There was nothing to do but stand around waiting for
her to finish her business. That got on Russo's nerves
and sometimes made him yank the leash.

Most days I went straight home. Outside my room
the last few sycamore leaves hung on like tiny torn um-
brellas, and the seed balls swayed in the wind. I was
painting and putting the decals now on the *U.S.S.
Missouri*, listening to my L.P. record of navy orchestra
music, *Victory at Sea*, and thinking of Margaret. For
Christmas I'd decided to get her a fan—the folding
Oriental kind, which moves in and out like a bellows.

Strange, how little I knew about Margaret. She
didn't seem to be an only child. What did her dad do?
Did she ever need a fan? One afternoon I called her
with several ways of asking stuff like that, but she was

in the middle of practice, so we didn't get far. Also, I was feeling jealous that day about Russo being so sure about things between himself and Patty. He knew they were bound to get married. I thought if Margaret and I were married, we might have more to talk about.

One afternoon Russo told me about confession—how the priest would get to sit in a big wooden box while parishioner knelt outside and talked. You couldn't see the priest inside the box, you could only talk through tiny holes. There were all kinds of sins to confess, like murder, swearing, coveting, meanness, or reading books like *Peyton Place*. Whatever sin you'd done, the priest would let you off if you said the same prayer over and over a number of times. The number was up to the priest. Russo was glad he hadn't done very much yet with Patty that might be called a mortal sin because, whatever he did, he'd need to tell the priest. For now he just did venial things, which sounded bad enough to me. But then the priest had pointed out that Patty wasn't Catholic, so Russo had better look out. Also, the priest didn't like peeking out and seeing Russo wearing his cross on the same chain as his half of the heart. That made Russo mad, which made the priest want to double his prayers until Russo backed off, saying he really controlled himself lately, in school and everywhere else. He also told the priest what I'd said about marrying someone for love. Of course, he hadn't yet told Pat about his plans for getting married. That could wait. He wanted to finish a little more school before they tied the knot.

One afternoon when the day stayed clear, he bugged her into meeting him by the pond at Chatham College. He wanted a snapshot of her to squeeze inside his ID bracelet. As usual, Margaret would be there, so this was my chance—if I wanted—to get a shot of her as well. I borrowed my parent's Kodak and together we walked up Chatham Road. The pond was at the foot of the slope below the college chapel. Patty and Margaret were already there, along with Patty's brother Ralph, who acted like we were nuts. He also kept kidding around with Margaret, grabbing the ends of her Allderdice scarf.

He said, "Hey, Arnold, get some trees in the background so you'll have something pretty to look at."

Russo took a picture of Patty leaning against an elm. For another, he wanted her to dangle her half of the heart with his, but she'd hadn't brought it even though she'd said she would. "Too shy" is how Russo summed her up. Then she and Margaret borrowed the camera and took some shots of us.

"Get one of Margaret with the ring," Russo told me.

But it wasn't the ring on the chain on her neck, just a cross she'd got at church. She hadn't brought the ring.

That upset Russo. He wanted me to chew her out the way he'd done to Patty.

"It's okay," I said.

"It's not okay," said Russo. "You gave her a ring, she should wear it!"

Ralph wandered back up to the chapel, up the steepest part of the hill where everyone sledded in winter. We hung around a while until the girls went home.

"What's with Pat?" I asked Russo as we walked back down to Fifth.

"Nothin'."

"She seemed kind of angry, even before you blamed her for not bringing her half of the heart."

He said, "Look, nothing happened!" After a while he added bleakly, "She's got a lot to learn."

"'Bout what?"

"Same things as you."

"Like what?"

"You name it."

"Tell me," I said.

"You wouldn't know if it walked up and bit you. You and Margaret? Jeez, wake me when it's over."

That night Margaret called.

"We need you to talk to Arnold," she said.

I was in the hall. Mom was nearby in the kitchen. Dad wasn't much farther away, in the living room reading. I slid into the closet among the coats.

"Why?" I said.

"Because she doesn't want to see him. And he's your friend," she said.

"Uh, should he call her instead?"

"No."

"Why not?"

"Because he's...he's been getting ahead of himself."

"How do you mean?"

"How do you think I mean?" she said.

"Oh."

"Will you tell him?" she asked.

"Okay."

"When?"

"I'll try and talk with him tomorrow."

"Thank you," she said.

I didn't want thanks. Not from Margaret. From her I wanted something not about Patty and Russo at all. I wanted one word about *us*. I squeezed myself deeper into the coats. What I really wanted to know was, if Russo wasn't seeing Patty, would I still be seeing Margaret?

"I have homework to finish," she said.

"You always have homework." I said, bothered.

"Well, don't you?" She sounded almost hurt. "And I need to finish practice."

"Okay."

"I do! We have the Christmas concert."

"Who?"

"The all-city junior-high. At the concert hall at Carnegie Museum." She'd talked herself into a corner. "Do you want to come?" she asked at last.

"Sure," I said. "When is it?"

"It's a Wednesday, the sixteenth."

"Sure, I'll come," I told her. "I'd be very glad to come."

"Okay. Well, see you then."

A brand-new me stepped out of the closet. The brilliant, beautiful Margaret, my Margaret, with my ring that she only wore in private, was playing a concert and wanted me there!

"Who was that?" asked Mom.

"Just Margaret."

I'd gone upstairs when she called back.

"Marty, please don't tell Arnold about the concert. See, Patty's coming."

"Sure."

What a traitor I am, I thought as we hung up. Not only had I agreed to lie about the concert. I had also agreed to do their dirty work of telling him he couldn't see Patty. What was I supposed to say? And was this forever or just for now? At least, why couldn't he call?

I couldn't do any more homework that night. I got lost again thinking about Margaret and the folding fan for Christmas. You could buy them in a five-and-ten, cheap, but that didn't sound very classy. I decided to get her a fan-shaped pin instead that I'd seen at the EZ Credit. Before my parents went to bed, I slipped into their room to call up Russo and give him the news.

"Who's this?" he answered.

"It's me," I said, "and Margaret called. She says Patty can't see you right now."

"What's that supposed to mean—right now?"

"I don't know," I said. "She wants to be alone or something."

"Who says? Her parents?"

"Them and her, I guess," I said.

He said, "Why did Margaret call you about this instead of Patricia calling me?"

"I don't know."

"Okay, I'll call her," he said.

"They don't want that either," I said.

"So why the hell not?"

"That's all I know," I said.

"What business is it of Margaret's?" he asked. "It don't concern Margaret any more than you."

I could tell he'd known this was coming. I could almost hear the tears.

"This is great," he said and hung up.

Then he tried to call Patty, is what he told me next morning at school. But she wouldn't answer the phone herself, and none of her family would put her on.

A few nights later, Margaret called again and told me, "Marty, tell Arnold to stop."

7

Russo was mad at Patty for giving in to her parents. One day in early December, he cut the afternoon of school to have more time to get up there on foot and catch her coming home. There he stood in freezing rain until she came and she and Margaret walked by like they didn't even see him.

He played hooky a few more days after that. When he did show up at school again, Mrs. Heiler said he must have come down with something—that was how gloomy he was. And she was right: he'd come way down with love. But a few days later his mood let up. Now he said now he understood the Colbys. He just had to show he loved her. Also, turning Protestant should give him a much better chance. He went downtown to the Kaufmann's department store and bought her a sweater for Christmas. He planned to drop it off before he left for New Jersey, where he had to spend the holidays. Just drop it off—not even ask to step inside and see her. He said I was lucky to have a girl with folks as easy as Margaret's. He made me feel a little guilty.

In a way he was relieved, because now he had more time to scrounge up the money he needed, with Christmas, barely two weeks away. He was getting up at five in the morning to go to the alley where the paperboys picked up their papers, in case one of them didn't show up and the man might let Russo fill in. But paperboys don't get sick around Christmas: that's when they make their biggest tips.

He had a key from Sherry now. After school he'd let himself into her apartment and do the dishes she'd left from breakfast and the night before and straighten up her rooms. He washed her windows, and some neighbors' windows, too, for free, and they paid him in tips. The last week before vacation, he got night work at a gas station and fell asleep in class, even knowing how Mrs. Heiler would sneak around and snap her ruler on his neck.

"You're a disgrace," she told him. "Yes, lower your head! Do you know where your life is going, Mr. Sixteen? I'll tell you where you're heading. Kids giggled but Russo went red, slinking lower in his seat. Later he was mad because, he said, she'd been wrong. He wasn't sixteen. He wouldn't be sixteen until December 28. And Veronica Hilly was fifteen, too, and sat there halfway napping. Why didn't she get picked on, too?

"Wanna know why I'm in eighth grade?" he asked.

I wasn't sure I did.

"Because they think I'm dumb," he said.

"I don't," I said. Well, in some ways I did, but he wasn't asking for truth on a Bible.

"Because dumb in school is dumb, right? Right?"

He pushed me to confess. Then he told me again about all the husbands his mother had had and all the places they'd moved around. He'd been born in Texas, where his dad and mom had got married a week before Pearl Harbor. His mother's name was Dorothy, but they called her Dotty. Then Russo's dad joined the Merchant Marine, after the navy wouldn't take him, so

Dotty took Bunny and little Arnold, who was two, back to her family in Scranton, PA. They moved to Baltimore and from there to Cherry Hill, Delaware and from there to Campton, New Jersey. By that time the mom was married again. As Russo said, she just kept "signing on the dottied line." (*Ha ha.*) But every time they moved, Arnie was set back in school because he wasn't keeping up. He'd missed a lot of stuff they taught, but as time went by, he also got better at guessing answers on a test. Only he spelled so bad, his answers never counted. That's what he said. After Dotty went to Nevada and got her last divorce, she came back east and married Smitty Meacham. That was the stepdad that Russo had liked. Old Smitty had been a boilermaker in a navy shipyard and was deaf from banging on all those pipes, and he had some grownup kids of his own that led to trouble when he died about who got what. Plus now there was Little Smitty who was six and Dotty babied all the time and got mad if Russo even touched him. Now his mother was trying to marry a Greek with a very long name that started with T. The name was so long that all they called him was "Mr. T."

Mr. T. hadn't proposed yet. She was hoping he'd pop the question this Christmas, if she played her cards right and everyone including Russo pretended they liked eating sour grape leaves stuffed with rice. Russo didn't like Mr. T. He still wished Old Smitty was around because, for one thing Smitty had taught him how to drive. All he needed now was the license which you had to be sixteen to get.

I was pretty amazed at Russo's life. And I noticed how much he'd talk about Smitty instead of his own, real dad. There didn't seem to be much more to his father than that pea coat and the dog-eared photo in the trunk.

At supper that night I got to thinking how most stories start out about some kid whose parents are missing or dead. *Treasure Island* is like that. So is *Tom Sawyer*, and *Homer Price*. Pam says the same about *Anne of Green Gables*. It got me thinking, if one or even both my parents died, it would be sad but also kind of interesting. I wasn't complaining, exactly, but Russo did have room to do some things I couldn't do.

When school let out for the holidays, Russo wanted me to go downtown with him to the Greyhound, but Margaret's concert was that evening. I did help him carry his bags to the trolley. He had a mountain of presents. He even had presents for Big Smitty's children, who'd taken all the old man's dough.

He gave me the sweater for Patty (wrapped) and asked me to run it by her house. Then I told him about the concert, like I hadn't remembered until right then. The streetcar came and he was gone. I thought it was good because the trip might take his mind off Patty.

I wore my red blazer that night, and because it was the yuletide season Mom gave me a tie with little Rudolph reindeers. It was corny, but at least she didn't make me wear her Santa's helper hat, *ha ha*. The Hatfields came by to pick me up, since Margaret was already down at the hall. They didn't say much. I sat in the backseat with Russo's present for Patty and mine for Margaret in a bag on my lap. I'd bought her a hand-painted, rice-paper fan. (The gift shop man had said, "If you get hungry you can eat it.") The hand-painted part was a bright green bug sitting on a bamboo plant. It had only cost sixty-nine cents, so I'd also bought her some clip-on metal butterflies. They were also made in Japan, and cost a dime apiece. Instead of a pin, they had a spring that opened the butterfly's metal legs to latch them onto your clothes.

The Colbys and Patty were there at the concert. We saved a seat for Margaret for the second half when the senior orchestra played. I was wondering whether she might have eyes for one of the other players, and I was kicking myself for being a hick about classical music, apart from two or three short songs by Ludwig and Bach that Mr. Marjavi had thrown my way.

When Margaret walked out on stage, at first she looked about twenty years old. The music was good, though she didn't have any solos. At the intermission she came out while the senior orchestra got set up. A short while later, there was Ralph Colby up there, playing a rounded horn with his hand jammed up the end where the sound came out. I asked Margaret why he did that—he was always clowning around—but she informed me that's how French horns are supposed to be played. When Ralph played his solo, it sounded like a hunter chasing down some big gray wolf.

"So difficult!" said Margaret's mother as we clapped. Margaret beamed like she was up there herself.

After the concert there was punch and cookies in the lobby. Margaret went off and left me standing with some of her orchestra mates, all congratulating each other on how great the concert had been. There they were, standing around in their black pants or skirts, white shirts and black ties, white blouses with black bows, and there was I in my fire truck blazer and a green tie trimmed with red-nosed reindeer.

"Are you an elf?" some kid with heavy glasses asked. I moved away. The next group I ran into was deciding who was the greatest composer ever, and someone said Bach and I said, "Oh, yeah, I've played a few of his." Someone asked me what instrument I played and, when I told them what, they laughed and another girl said, "You play Bach on a concertina? Why?" I left that group as well. All around me they were cooing at each other, saying, *My dahling, you nevah played better*, and *Dahling, you were divine!*

I took some punch to Margaret but could tell she didn't want me hanging on, so I made some excuse and went off and found Patty who'd been wandering around. She was glad to see me up to the point I told her there was something for her in the coatroom from Russo. Then she didn't want it. I said I couldn't take it back and told her where to find it. Then I found Margaret and said I had something to give her before I left.

"I have something for you, too," she said as we walked to the coats.

All I could think it might be was a pair of men's gloves she'd admired with me window-shopping—gray leather lined with rabbit fur. But I'd also mentioned them to my folks, and I didn't need two pairs.

Russo's present was still on the shelf above the coats, but Patty must have already come in because the card was torn away. (For all I know, that sweater's still there, waiting for some better Christmas.) I got the fan out from under my coat and held it out to Margaret. She unwrapped it and said, "It's nice."

I reached in my pocket to fish out the butterflies, which I hadn't thought needed wrapping. As I did, she held out the thunderbird ring and said, "I need to give this back."

"You don't need to give it back," I said.

"Please take it."

"No, it's yours."

She followed me out of the coatroom.

"It was a great concert," I heard me say. "Say thanks to your parents. Say hi to Patty. Are you doing anything for Christmas?"

She glanced around like she didn't want anyone else to hear this going on between us. Then she said, "Patty really likes you."

I walked the two miles home. I walked a block or so before I even realized it was cold. I started singing Christmas carols, and for me, once they were sung, my Christmas was already over.

"What makes you so grouchy?" Pammy asked.

"What makes you so nebby?" I replied.

We were doing the usual holiday stuff—candles, stockings, cookies, trees. The only new thing about it was Dad went to tbe beer distributor and bought some KDKA-radio, Rege-Cordek-and-Company Frothing-slosh, "the pale stale ale with the foam on the bottom." We drove through the South Hills one night where people went bonkers with lights in their yards and plywood Santas on the roof. There wasn't any snow.

"Where's the funeral?" Dad asked.

For Christmas I got a logan coat with a hood and antler-tip toggles. The cloth was twice as thick as Russo's pea coat, so stiff that it practically stood by itself. I got the gloves I'd seen downtown on my first and last date with Margaret (not from Margaret, from my folks) and the speedometer I no longer wanted. My dad had parked our brand-new '58 Rambler out front with a huge red bow on the roof, and I didn't even care about that.

I also got a plastic kit for the *U.S.S. Hornet*, which as Dad pointed out was the aircraft carrier that had brought Jimmy Doolittle's bombers into striking range of Tokyo. It was amazing how little my parents knew about me anymore, as though I planned to go on building plastic models all my life. I sat at my window, drumming my fingers on the box of 252 gray plastic pieces and missing beautiful, deadly Margaret. The day after Christmas, Mom got out the sew-on labels she'd used three years before to mark my clothes for the Boy Scout camp they'd made me try. She sewed my name into one of my gloves and dragged me downtown, hunting for bargains. That evening she and Dad and Pam walked up to the Greenbaums' for a Hanukkah party. I stayed home.

"Where *is* that funeral?" asked Mom.

What to do alone all evening? There was nothing on TV, no one to call, no Margaret, no Russo. I tried re-reading *Call of the Wild* and couldn't get past page three. Around midnight, after they came back, I dumped the *Hornet* parts out on my bed, turned on the lamp, broke a bunch of them off their stems and sloppily started to glue. I fell asleep, woke up the morning after Christmas and went on gluing more and more of it together. There was something right about mindlessly gluing all those stupid pieces. At noon I finally went down to eat.

"It's snowing," Mom pointed out, like that should make a difference. Outside the kitchen window, it fell in little waffles. That meant the air was wet and the snow would crunch and be good for snowballs and sleds. It was already sticking.

I went up again, closed myself in, and went on gluing like a war was on. I imagined Russo's old stepdad, Smitty Meacham, the boilermaker, down below deck, banging away on the pipes. Mom brought up soup.

"It smells like a dope den in here," she said. She sniffed the glue. "Mister, we're getting you out."

When I said I wasn't going, she opened the curtain and raised the sash. The snow was an inch deep on the roof. She said it was deeper on the walk.

About three o'clock she came back and said, "Out." She handed me the marmalade she'd wrapped to give to the Marjavis. "And that's an order."

Okay, I got dressed, went down, climbed inside my brand new duffel coat (a really good coat, I must say), and crossed the street and rang their bell. No one answered. They could have been out shopping for food, which they often did together, or maybe were at the drugstore getting more prescriptions for him. I didn't feel like waiting around, but if I left their present outside the door, the mailman might think it was for him, so I stuffed the jar in a pocket and started back across the street. The snow was about two or three inches and already made a subtle crunch. Halfway across, I knew I didn't want to go back in the house, not even to get my boots, so I started walking over toward Highland Avenue, walking the empty street. As I crossed Highland, kids were hurrying up toward the college with flying saucers and sleds. I joined the crowd a block or so but when they turned up Chatham Road, the thought of running into someone made me stop. The air was snow-warm, wet and sweet like it only ever is in Pittsburgh when a heavy snow is falling. A Studebaker went by along Fifth, slowly—a newer model than the '50. Some teenage daredevil ran out, dove to a crouch hanging onto the bumper and slid away on his heels through the snow.

Paradise was wrapped in snow. Another hour or so might pass before someone ruined it making snowmen. At the top of the lot, I pulled up my hood, put on my cozy rabbit gloves, and made an angel in the snow, which got a lot of snow up my socks. I stared up into the flaking sky, then wandered down to the stairway to nowhere, ate some frosting from the steps, and swept the top of it clean with my glove. Along Kentucky, a car went by, chains jingling on its wheels. It made me almost happy.

I was getting cold and about to leave when I glanced toward the naked crabapple tree and saw what looked like a marshmallow stuck to the trunk where I'd seen the locust last fall. It was snow that had piled on the top end of the empty shell. How strange to see the shell still hanging on there, pushing a marshmallow up the tree. Even when I flicked off the snow, the shell still clung, locked on by its insect legs. Its vacant turret eyes stared upward along the trunk it never got to climb. There I am, I thought, that's me. Don't know when he's licked. I bared a hand and picked off the shell and cradled it in my palm. A piece of popcorn might have weighed more.

By the time I was back at the Marjavis', the snow was another half inch deep. Mrs. Marjavi opened the door, saw my sodden feet and asked what in the world I was doing out without galoshes. Inside, she made me take off my shoes. She took my socks as well and set them on the radiator. Meanwhile, she and Mr. Marjavi were about to have egg nog, so they made me stay and have some, too, without the whisky they'd put in their own.

"You hurt your hand?" asked Mr. M as I joined him at the kitchen table. He thought that was why my hand was curled up. I opened it to show him the shell. He took off his glasses for a look and said, "What else you get for Christmas?"

After that he said he was sorry he'd needed to cancel several lessons last fall on account of his health. He had some trouble with his breathing that had made him give up cigarettes.

"Except when you can't resist," said his wife, "and then you pay for it good."

If he smoked even one, he'd wheeze all night. Even the splash of whisky in his egg nog made him take out his hanky and cough until she rubbed his back.

"By the way," he said, "your friend Arnie called to wish us season's greetings."

"He did?" I said. That worried me. As far as I'd been aware, Russo didn't even know them, though I'd probably mentioned their name. I was going to ask more about that when Mr. Marjavi started remembering places he used to play on Polish Hill, some Italian restaurants in Bloomfield, and various taverns in the steelworker towns along the Monongahela River. One of his favorites happened to be a tie-up for boaters on the Allegheny, called Thunderbird Lodge.

That made me wish I'd given *him* the ring.

Mrs. Marjavi talked about how Ed Sullivan used to have more accordions on his Sunday night show from New York.

I told them about the concert—not about Margaret but about the snooty girl who'd asked me *Why*. Mrs. M threw up her hands.

Mr. M nodded and said, "You know, Marty, when people make fun of accordions, it has nothing to do with the instrument we happen to play. It's the fault of too many accordion players who make it sound like the merry-go-round at Kennywood Park by thinking all they need to do is seesaw the bellows back and forth. That's the ones who never really play the accordion, instead the accordion plays *them*."

"Same as life," said Mrs. M, like she was talking to no one.

"That's what I'm training you not to do," Mr. Marjavi continued, "so you won't play crapola like them. Violins sound terrible, too, if the fiddler don't know how to bow. And maybe sounding good comes easier on a violin because most people happen to be right-handed and the right arm does the bowing. For us, it's the bellows, all over there."

He poked my left arm.

"I know," I said, not because I really knew but because I wanted to know. "The problem is, the melody keys are on the right, and whatever I try to do on the left side with the bellows gets swallowed up by the bass notes I'm hitting on the left. I get confused in between—"

"No!" he interrupted. "It's only the *fingers* that pick out the chords. It's your *arm* that's got to *play*. Your

105

left arm makes the sahnd. Get that left arm into the act to say what you want to say."

"But I'm right-handed, so half the time, I can't even feel what my left arm's doing. So how do I play all emotional if—?"

"Emotional is not what I'm saying!" He coughed again and wrapped up his spit in order to go on. "Decide how what you want to say with your music and get that left arm working on that. (*Cough, wipe.*) The bellows, my boy, the wind, your life! (*Snort.*) Think more about where your expression might come from, how different parts of you could express (*cough*)—even invisible parts of yourself, which is what most left arms happen to be. Things you never (*cough, snort, wheeze, wipe*) thought about before. Sign up at the Boys' Club for boxing. You'll find aht what a left arm is!"

Mrs. M poked him and said, "Now, Marty, he don't mean that, abaht you need to learn to box."

"Maybe I do," Mr. M growled back. "Got it, Marty?" He tapped my arm again.

"Okay."

"Don't leave that left arm out of your life."

"I won't," I said, still wondering how.

"Babe," he said to Mrs. Marjavi, pointing into his half-empty mug. "Wanna add some more of the good stuff?"

"No," she said, "but I will, or else you'll go on and add more than me." She added another splash of the booze.

Then Mr. Marjavi started coughing like he always did when he talked too much, and Mrs. Marjavi looked at his hanky and scurried to get him a couple of clean ones.

"My wife," he said. "She keeps me livin'."

"More nog for you, Marty?" she asked.

That night Russo called from New Jersey. I could barely hear him over the bad connection and a roar of trucks outside the phone booth. Even in my parents' room, I had to listen hard.

"So," he said, "they dumped us."

"Who told you that?" I said, wondering how he knew to say "us"—like the news had somehow reached him about Margaret and the ring.

"Pat. Been calling her every day till now. She says don't bother calling no more." A truck roared by, and he added, "Well, like ol' Brando says, 'Sayonara, sucker.'"

"I guess you're right," I said, though I didn't remember Brando's saying that exactly. I just wanted to agree.

"Well, it's sure nice weather here in the Garden State," he went on. "Been snowin' and meltin' all week. We got us a nice lot of slush."

"Where are you?" I asked.

"Service station near the house. Nice place, open late. Need any gas? I'll pour some to ya through the line." Another truck went by. "I'm too old for precious Patty."

"Well," I tried to sound consoling, "you might need someone older."

The operator cut in and asked for more money. Russo said, "Hey, babe, you busy tonight?"

"Please deposit seventy cents," she said. I heard him feeding the coins.

"At least I'm gettin' outta here," he said. "My half-half brother Crosley's takin' me along to Baltimore. He drives for Wilby's Pies. He's teachin' me how to drive his truck. 'Take me along,' I says. 'I'll keep you awake so both of us won't get killed.'"

"Hope not," I said.

"Better than dyin' alone. So wish me happy birthday."

"Really? When?"

"Day after tomorrow. We'll stop on the road somewhere and order candles with our soup."

"Happy birthday," I said.

"So mail me a party," he said.

The operator cut in for more money. At that point, Russo hung up. I hung up, too, and thought about his turning sixteen and how he really did need a girlfriend older than Patty Colby. Too bad Veronica was taken.

"Who's calling so late?" Dad asked as I headed upstairs.

"Russo."

"How's he doing?" asked Mom.

"Okay. Just sad about his birthday."

"I thought he's with his family," she said.

"That's the problem," I said.

Russo came back before the new year. We invited him over for supper. He talked all through dinner, asking how Mom made such creamy potatoes and she told him her secret was eggs. He told her how to know when spaghetti was done.

"Throw a piece of it at the wall," he said. "If it sticks, it's done. If it don't, throw it back in the pot with the rest."

She liked that. Dad asked if the same test worked for mashed potatoes. We had a good time, and Russo cried when she brought out the cake. Singing the words of "Happy Birthday" was the only time I ever called him Arnold to his face.

Later, up in my room, I gave him the photos of Patty I'd finally picked up from the pharmacy. He barely looked. Instead he talked about all the things he'd never liked about her, and we debated what he should do if or when she ever wanted him back. I didn't mention Margaret's telling me how Patty liked me better. And I didn't show him the pictures of Margaret. I didn't want him to badmouth her along with Patty. There was nothing I wanted to hear.

He never told me any more about all that had happened in Jersey.

After the new year Russo started clowning around at school. It was like a disease he'd caught on vacation. It started one afternoon when Mrs. Hitler left the room at her usual time.

As soon as the door closed, Russo piped up, "Goodbye, teacher. Too bad you ain't good enough to teach high school." That got a nervous laugh. Next day when she went out, he said, "I saw somethin' peachy on the television set last night—the goldfish bowl." That got a snicker here and there.

Sometimes he ran through three or four jokes before he got a good enough laugh. When he didn't get the laugh, he couldn't give up trying. Once everyone caught on to that, they starting holding back. No joke was funnier than watching Russo squirm for the laugh. Plus, then he switched to dirtier jokes, which meant you had to laugh whether you got it or not, so you wouldn't look like you didn't.

One day it was, "Did everyone hear about the absent-minded professor? He unbuttoned his vest, pulled out his tie and wet his pants." That one kept some of us cracking up all afternoon, with Mrs. Heiler right there wondering what was going on.

Another day he told a somehow dirty joke about Marilyn Monroe. It was something to do with "Joltin' Joe" DiMaggio, the New York Yankee who was married to her until she divorced him for being so mean. It wasn't all that funny, but we began to laugh anyway until Veronica jumped up in his face and said, "Don't you talk abaht her!"

That shut us up, especially considering since Veronica could tell some spicey jokes herself. We all knew something was wrong with *this* one, as far as she was concerned.

We were still dead silent when Mrs. Heiler came back in and said, "Well, for once you're quiet."

We never knew how Mrs. Heiler caught onto all his shenanigans behind her back. As mad as Veronica was that time, she'd never rat on anyone. Whoever it was that squealed, Russo was sent to the office where Miss Giltenbooth paddled him again and warned him not to tempt her and Mrs. Heiler to make him serve another year in grade school.

He apologized to Veronica, and the two of them made up, but his clowning put distance between us. After the paddling he started to pal around with another kid in our class who hated school and was always being sent to the office. Me, I drifted back to Bing and the guys, even if they still did razz me now and then.

One afternoon I had a choice between shoveling walks with Russo or sledding up on Chatham Road, and I went sledding. The college girls slid down the hill on cafeteria trays. Wesley was riding a new kind of skis—one ski with a seat and handlebars—that always dumped him off. Now he and Bing were trying to talk some college students into getting on the ski with them, and then they'd make it crash.

"Who you looking for?" Snyder asked me when I looked around.

"No one," I said, half hoping, half dreading Margaret might show up. "So who are you?" I asked.

"He's lookin' for his Chink," said Bing.

"I am?" said Wesley.

"Who are you talking about?" I said.

"Wesley's got a crush on her," said Bing. "She lives around here somewhere. Cute."

"Yeah, right," said Wesley, as though Bing had accused him of having a crush on Mrs. Heiler.

I looked around for a girl that might be Chinese.

"She was sledding?" I asked.

"Not today," said Bing. "Anyway, she's kinda young."

"That wouldn't matter to Russo," said Wesley. "He likes 'em young."

"Never mind," I said, and took my last run of the day.

Then a weird thing happened. I was over by the little pond, which Wesley said had never frozen thick enough this year for hockey. It never froze very solid except when the weather was really cold. Another problem was a feeder pipe that dribbled water up into the middle of the pond, which meant the ice out there stayed thinner than the rest. The whole pond was only about fifty feet long and fifteen feet across. I was standing at the edge, looking at bubbles trapped in the ice when a large twig landed on my head.

Above, in the tips of an elm, two squirrels were chasing each other around. Then another little branch snapped off and suddenly one of the squirrels was hanging on to tiny ends of things, all about to break away. It was comical until it fell.

I ducked. The squirrel fell about thirty feet. It

didn't land on me, but on the pond beside the feeder pipe. I saw the splash. Then it started madly grabbing around between the broken bits of ice, to climb out on its belly. But pretty soon I knew it wasn't making it out.

It was six or eight feet out from me, and I had no idea how deep the water was. I did know that you couldn't walk out on that ice. Finally I ran around the edge of the pond to tear off part of a bush that I could maybe slide out for the squirrel to grab, but I couldn't break it off. Meanwhile the poor wet squirrel was churning up a storm.

"Guys!" I yelled for help, but no one looked my way. Then, as I searched around for something else it could grab, that weird French Greenbaum car pulled up and Mr. Greenbaum got out.

"What's the trouble?" he asked, but by that time he already saw for himself.

When he saw what I was trying to do, he also grabbed the bush and both of us yanked, and the thing tore off at the roots.

"I'll throw," he said, and did, and the branches landed where we wanted. Eventually, the squirrel shinnied up, and skittered off the ice. With its tail all wet, it looked like a rat. It scampered up the tree again and disappeared from view.

"Nice job," said Mr. Greenbaum. "Oh, aren't you Marty?"

"Yeah." I nodded. "You work with my dad."

"Right. Great to meet you, Marty. You all right? Want to stop by our place and get warm?"

"No thanks. That got me warm enough," I said.

"Sorry you couldn't be with us for Hanukkah last month. The kids were hoping to meet you," he said.

113

"I know, I was sorry, too," I lied.

We went back to the car and he showed me a couple things about it. Then he drove off further up the road, and I headed home with my sled. I couldn't stop wondering what those two squirrels had been doing up there in the middle of winter. Had they been mating? Up there? Wow.

Sure I'm crazy, Major, crazy in love!

"**H**ow come you don't come over no more?" Russo asked me. So I went. His place was about the same. Bunny's old boyfriend's picture was gone. In its place was a new one of a guy called Herbie.

"He looks fat," I said.

"He should," said Russo. "He's always moochin' off us."

We were down in the basement, where Russo was spending more and more time. He'd turned the storage cage into more of a room by painting the slats and spreading carpet on the floor. He had a canvas lawn chair now, along with the smelly, overstuffed chair. The furnace gave some heat. He was using two crates for a table where his radio sat, its cord running up to a double socket where the light attached. He turned on WEEP and Porky Chadwick—"your Daddy-o of the Raddy-o"— and held up a can of fruit cocktail and another of pork and beans.

"Take your pick," he said.

Soon the beans were heating on the furnace.

"Sherry lets you stay down here?" I asked.

"Oh, yeah, she knows. I told her myself. Besides, I sweep the basement, free, and mop sometimes. Plus the stairs and landings. You name it, that's what I do."

He was being paid a little in cash, plus Sherry kept thinking about taking something off Bunny's rent. He liked talking to Sherry, he said. She understood the troubles he'd been having, and she backed up the chorus of voices telling him Patty was way too inexperienced for someone Russo's age. He batted the *Playboy* down from my face and turned the music off.

"Listen." He hummed a tune. "Hear that?" he said and hummed some more.

Down there in the basement he sounded great. He strapped his big accordion on, perched at the edge of the chair and played what sounded a little like Johnny Mathis's "Chances Are." He missed a ton of notes, but I thought he'd made a little progress. He couldn't play and sing at the same time, so he tried to make me sing, but my voice had been changing and the key he played in didn't fit where I could sing.

I asked why he'd called the Marjavis at Christmas. I'd forgotten even having pointed out to him where they lived. He said he'd gone over a couple times for lessons. It was easy because he didn't need to bring his accordion. He could use one of Mr. M's loaners.

But why did you do it behind my back? I asked.

"Not on account of you," he explained. "The reason's because your parents might feel bad if they knew I got some lessons free. Okay, let's sing together."

We settled on a song by Patience and Prudence, their duet "Tonight You Belong to Me." He sang one part, I sang the other. The words went about like this:

> Patience (him):   *I know...*
> Prudence (me):   *I know...*
> Patience (him):   *You be-long...*

115

Prudence (me):	*be-lo-o-o-ong...*
Patience (him):	*To some-...*
Prudence (me):	*so-o-o-o-ome-...*
Patience (him):	*body new...*
Prudence (me):	*ne-e-e-e-ew...*
Patience (him):	*But tonight...*
Prudence (me):	*But tonight...*
Both of us:	*You be-lo-ong*
	To me.
Me:	*Just to little old me.*

Over beans, we discussed how to launch ourselves as a duo, as soon one or the other could sing at the same time as play. First, what we needed was a name.

"How 'bout *Martin and Arnold*?" I suggested.

"Naw."

"*Marty and Russo*?"

He waved that away.

"*The Cavalier Brothers*," he said.

"I dunno."

"*The Playboys*."

"No. My mother would shoot me."

"*Marteeny and Russo*."

"No."

"Come on," he said. "It makes you sound Italian. All good singers are Italians."

"Too bad," I said.

When we came upstairs, it was going on five and starting to get dark. The phone rang. Russo answered, hung up and said, "That was Sherry. She wants us to take out the dog before she gets home, so it don't go potty in the kitchen."

I felt strange entering Sherry's apartment. Her

curtains were drawn, and the place was almost totally dark. But Russo knew where he was going. He crossed and turned on a lamp.

"She don't use the ceiling lights," he said. "Too gloomy."

He'd brought up her paper and laid it on the coffee table. The living room sofa sat in a cozy pool of light. I pictured Mrs. Sheridan coming home and stretching out. A shelf nearby held glasses and bottles. Did she have a drink every night? On the arm of the sofa, a beanbag ashtray held cigarette butts with filters and lipstick marks.

Russo seemed to read my mind. He sighed and said. "She'll come home, take her coat off, turn on the TV, sit here, take her shoes off, put her feet up, read the paper...."

Edith the spindly poodle was yapping. It skidded across the linoleum as Russo took something out of the fridge. I held her on her leash while he brought a pair of Chinese slippers from the bedroom and put them next to the sofa. He took one last look around and said, "Another happy customer."

Outside, a lady was coming. "That's her," he said. "Don't say you was up there."

It was Sherry on this mild winter evening. She was wearing a poodly coat with a paisley scarf on her head. Edith jumped all over her as Russo introduced her ("Mrs. Sheridan") to me. Without the glove, her hand was pink and soft.

"I'm pleased to meet you, Marty," she said.

In the light of the front steps, the ends of her hair were pale. Her eyes seemed to bulge from her face a little more than other people. She held my hand a little long. *What had Russo told me about her?* she wanted to

117

know with a friendly smile. Then she let me go and asked Russo if he wouldn't mind keeping Edith out a little longer.

"Can you believe she's forty?" he said when she'd gone in.

He meant Sherry, not Edith, but either way I wasn't sure how young or old he meant forty to sound like it was.

At supper Mom asked where I'd been so late. She'd called Russo's and got no answer. I told her we'd been in the basement. I didn't mention sneaking up to Sherry's, but Mom was onto something.

"Why don't you hang out more with Wesley?" she asked. "His mother says they've put up a basketball hoop in the drive."

Sometimes Russo complained about how Sherry was asking him to do more and more, like when a lightbulb went out or touching up the paint in the hall. At the same time, he was doing things she never asked him to do, like keeping a certain number of candies and cigarettes in the bowls on the coffee table or fiddling with the silver lighter so it always lit. He was spending more and more time up there. He also bought a folding cot at the army-navy store so he could sleep in the basement when Herbie stayed over with Bunny.

"It stinks," he complained. "And sometimes I can't even use the toilet!"

I did not ask, in that case, what he did.

Around the end of January we were going to supper at the Greenbaums. Mrs. Greenbaum was making something special. I knew what chopsticks were, of course, but I'd sever seen Japanese food. I wondered how Mr. Greenbaum's wife would know anything about it either until we pulled up at their house. Even in the dark I could see it was different than most houses in Pittsburgh, even different from most on Chatham Road. It was low and spread out so you'd hardly notice it was there. A path of stones led up to the door. The front door opened, a little kid looked out, looked up in my face and said, "Hi."

He looked familiar though I couldn't say from where until his mother came up behind him and looked out and said, "Welcome. Reggie, let the Badgers in."

It all came back to me then—the crazy kid at Paradise, "Bombs away" and all—and there was his mother who was making Japanese food because she was Japanese or something doggone close. She didn't sound Japanese, just looked it, but I knew then what a terrible night I was in for if Reggie had really recognized me and said anything about what I'd said that night last fall about wiping out Japs. But then we were all inside and there was Mr. Greenbaum shaking hands with Dad and taking our coats and passing them back to Reggie's littler sister and the Greenbaum's seventh grader. Only she wasn't a boy and wasn't *Nicky*, *N-I-C-K-Y*, I later found out, but *Nikki*, *N-I-K-K-I*.

Then Reggie was whispering something in Mrs. Greenbaum's ear to which she whispered back and shuffled him off to the kitchen.

Something smelled like sweetened smoke. "Smell that?" asked Dad. "That's teriyaki barbecue."

And the next thing on the spit would be me.

But then we all sat down to eat, and for the rest of that night not a word was said about bombs, and I hoped to heck it never would be, because I liked these people, including this Nikki, this friend of my sister, this pretty seventh-grade girl. I don't know if she looked more Japanese like Mrs. Greenbaum or more Jewish like her father, or somewhere in between, but after that I took every chance I could to glance at her lively, small round face.

So the Greenbaum kids were Nikki and her little brother Reggie, whose name in Japanese was *R-E-I-J-I* and the little sister they called Tommy, whose real name was Tomoko which means "wisdom," which is a funny name for a five-year-old who only wants people's attention. And we fumbled around so much my mother asked if we could eat with forks. Me, I didn't switch because Pammy had already been there once and said she was almost used to chopsticks which she wasn't but I couldn't let her show me up. The most embarrassing moment that night was when Mr. Greenbaum, who swore he wasn't making fun, had to tell the story of saving the squirrel.

"But how did it fall?" Nikki asked when everyone stopped laughing.

"I don't know," I hedged. "I guess they were chasing each other around."

"Don't squirrels hibernate in winter?" said my foolish, know-it-all sister.

"No," said Mrs. G. "At least not all winter. They have to get out to eat. And mate."

"Mom!" said Nikki.

Mom said, "Really? In winter they mate?"

Mrs. G turned to Nikki and said. "Well, that's what you wrote in your school report. So the kits can be born in the spring."

"Marty, tell them about the nature house at Frick," said Mom, then turned to Sumi Greenbaum (Nikki's mother) and asked, "Do you ever go to Frick Park?"

Frick Park was long, public woodsy ravine that, like everything else it seemed, was up and over Squirrel Hill. It turned out they spent whole afternoons hiking around on its trails, catching insects and poison ivy.

That whole evening was amazing. Inside, too, their house was different from ours—warm and with shadows that didn't feel gloomy. A fire burned on a fireplace and here and there corners of rooms sat in puddles of light that glowed through rice-paper screens. There were rugs here and there, but the floor was concrete—red and smooth—and the heat came up through the floor. You could lie down and feel it come up.

Part of me wanted to talk with Nikki. Another part was glad just not to wreck the night. Pammy kept letting all of us know that Nikki was *her* friend (that's probably why she'd never said a word about her), taking her away to talk; or else the grownups were around all the time until the evening was over, and the Greenbaums were walking us out. By their garage sat three or four big glass jars. I asked what they were for and Mr. Greenbaum said they were from the Heinz factory downtown, and most of them used to hold pickles.

"That's not what's in them now," said Nikki.

She set one next to a light in the drive. Inside was a bunch of twigs with bits of fluff stuck on. She'd collected them last fall. They were cocoons. Her father said she planned to see what came out of each one in the spring. Then she planned to unravel the white stuff and see if it was silk, like the scarf around my neck.

If only she'd been older!

I found myself thinking about her a lot, though when Bing would ask me what was going on between me and Margaret I'd just say, "Not much," not letting on we'd broken up. But he probably knew. I'd still think of calling her now and then, but let the days go by.

One afternoon when I came home a little late, there were Nikki and Pammy, stretched out on Pam's bed, reading. Up to now, this had been my sister's only goal in life: to get some slightly older girl than she was to come and hang out, so I shouldn't have been surprised. Nikki was in blue jeans with her shirt tails out, her thick dark hair in a ponytail with wisps down the sides of her face. I stuck my head in, saying *hi*. She smiled, looking really cute. Then I turned to my room and bit my lip at having left my own door open, since Nikki must have glanced inside. If she had, then what she must have seen was a plastic Grumman Hellcat fighter hanging from the ceiling, chasing a balsa-stick Japanese Zero. (The Hellcat fighters had flown off the *U.S.S. Hornet*, which was sitting on my desk. What a sloppy job I'd done on the *Hornet*!) Then there was the "Mighty Mo" with its cannons sticking out all over. She must think I secretly hated someone. I even had a photo of the A-bomb being loaded into the B-29 that had dropped it on Nagasaki. Quickly I closed myself in and threw my school stuff so I could start hiding all that crap. Before I got far came a knock and there was Nikki *asking* to look at my models. What could I say?

To make a joke, I pointed out the locust shell,

parked on the flight deck of the *Hornet* in among the fold-wing fighters.

"That's a locust shell," I said.

"I know," she said. "It's called a cicada. They leave it behind when they molt."

I don't know where she got the word *molt.* I'd only heard it used before about snake skins found in the woods. I also showed her the *U.S.S. Missouri* and the place on deck where my dad would watch through binoculars.

"He wasn't a gunner," I pointed out.

"Is that your accordion?" she asked, having spied the case.

I nodded, wondering how *she* knew that was what it was. Maybe Pammy had ratted me out.

"Play something," she said.

"Well, I'm playing new things now, and most of them are pretty hard."

"Play something simple."

I got it out and played her "Minka Minka," the Russian song we'd learned in fifth grade, in A-minor with chords I'd invented myself:

(A-minor) *From the Volga I was riding,*
(E7) *On my great horse nobly striding,*
(A-minor again) *When I saw in shadows hiding,*
(E7) *Minka, charming* (A-minor again!) *Minka!*

She said it sounded like the Tamburitzans and, before I could ask who they were, added "I saw you just before Christmas."

"You did?"

"At the orchestra party."

"At Carnegie?"

123

She nodded. "I play cello."

"I can't believe I didn't see you," I said. Or maybe I just hadn't noticed.

"You were talking with Margaret Hatfield," she said. "Next year she'll be in senior orchestra at school."

"And you'll be eighth grade."

"Seventh," she said.

"I meant next year," I said. "You're in seventh grade now."

"No, I'm in sixth," she said.

"Oh."

I tried to make that super-casual, meanwhile thinking, *Sixth grade? Sixth? Pammy's grade?!*

I didn't entirely catch her next few words—something about her uncle and an accordion he used to have. Her mother used to tell Nikki how he used to play it around the camp.

"They went to summer camp?" I asked.

"No." She paused. "Internment camp."

It's strange, the word *internment*. It sounds like getting buried, or like something that happened in between things, like the different seasons, and it took me a moment to remember where else I'd heard it. It was what they called the camps for the Nazi prisoners of war.

"They were soldiers?" I finally said.

She looked at me oddly. "No, it was a camp for families. For Japanese during the war. Here in this country. In the desert."

"Oh, yeah," I said. Of course I'd heard about that, just always thought they'd only happened out in California. Plus, I might not have heard them called *internment* camps. Now I didn't know what to say. I was sorry her uncle and mother had been sent to stockades in the desert, but I couldn't think how to say that and I'd heard somewhere that Japanese people had been sent there for their own protection. The only problem was they had to leave so much behind, and while they were all sitting out in the desert, the stuff they left behind was stolen.

"What kind of music did he play?" I said, to change the subject.

"He played for dances. For my mother and her friends, and other people in the camp."

"Japanese dances?"

"No, silly. Like Benny Goodman, music like that. Jitterbug and swing. He died before I was born."

Then neither of us knew what to say but only looked around until Pammy came and stole her back. Then Nikki's mother called to tell her to get on home. I was going to offer to walk her, but Pammy got there first by saying she'd walk her up to Fifth, which meant that if I walked Nikki further than that, I'd end up walking Pamela, too; and I didn't feel like walking both of them together. But as they left, I clipped a butterfly onto Nikki's coat and said it meant good luck.

When they were gone I still wondered why Nikki had asked if that was my accordion. She must have already known it was mine. Had someone in my family told her, the other night at supper? Had Pam let on just now? Or had Nikki overheard that awful conversation at the orchestra party? Or, worst of worst, was Nikki friends with Margaret, and had Margaret told her all about me? And then I thought how, if Margaret or Bing or anyone else knew I was any way, even slightly interested in Nikki, they'd call that pure pathetic. *Cradle robber!*—I could hear it. As if that's what I was up to. Which I wasn't. Then later again I got to thinking how this neighborhood of ours was in a sort of no-man's-land between Allderdice High School over the hill and Peabody, the other high school north of Shadyside about a mile where me and most Liberty kids would go, and all at once I wondered if I might be able to switch to Allderdice, and life might be a whole lot better. Except then I'd see Margaret in the halls, and she'd see me, and that would be murder. So again, like my sister, another girl had got there first.

A week or so later, I would say, was when the trouble really started. It didn't start like much. Arthur caught the flu, and old Miss Geesa asked me to stand in for him on Safety Patrol until Artie was back in school. I'd never raised my hand for Safety Patrol, so I felt too guilty to refuse. His intersection was down at the foot of the field, where Ivy crosses Ellsworth. Miss Geesa said it wouldn't last beyond a week, but it turned into more like three.

Two things, and two things only, I liked about being patrol boy. First, the little kids respected someone who could stick out their hand at a car. Second, you got out of school five minutes early to get to your post.

What I didn't like was having to stick around even after you were almost certain that all the Liberty kids had crossed. Kids from St. Vincent's, a Catholic grade school, would also use my crossings but never listened to me. The young ones weren't so bad, but try making a gang of thirteen-year-old Catholic school girls wait for a light. They were louder compared to the Liberty girls and all dressed alike in white blouses and ugly green skirts. They cracked their gum and stuck up their noses at public Safety Patrol boys wearing dinky white patrol belts.

Two boys from St. Vincent's that bothered me were a pair called Louie and Anthony. Neither of them was all that big, but they swaggered by like gangsters. Anthony looked almost normal, but Louie had a reptile look. One day they each lobbed slushballs at me as they sauntered toward me down the block. A first-grade girl got hit and cried and the slush got into her boot.

I asked them to stop. Politely.

"Shut up, punk!" they said, and shouldered me into the street. From the other side after they crossed, another slushball landed behind me. After that, they taunted and pushed me around every day. Then for a few days they didn't come by, and I thought I'd got rid of them, but the next afternoon I was standing there dreaming when a hard one hit me in the face. If patrol boys had machine guns, then and there I would have mowed them down. But on they came and pushed me again in the street.

I tried to act like nothing had happened, but Russo came by and asked me what had done that to my face.

"You should've fought it out," he lectured me. "No matter there was two of them. Buncha hoodlums. You could beat them."

That was dumb. First, it *did* matter there was two of them. Second, who knew if they carried knives? Russo told me forget about knives. He wanted me to choose whichever one I wanted to fight and he'd keep the other one out of it. But I didn't want to fight either one. If I did beat Louie—the more evil one of the two—they'd only come back and get me together. Plus I'd seen them once with Jimmy, Veronica's boyfriend, the duck-tailed guy with the Stoodie. I'd seen them go by in the back seat once with Veronica sitting up front.

Russo was philosophical about it. All he said was, "Well, you gotta get beat up sometime."

"Did that ever happen to you?" I asked.

He showed me a little scar on his chin and said, "Heck, old Smitty used a buckle."

"I meant by other kids," I said.

"Sure," he said. "Marty, you gotta' get even or they'll treat you like a dog forever."

I guessed he was right. Also, his idea for getting even didn't seem too risky to me. Next afternoon he came down to my post as soon as school let out and ducked into an alley on Ellsworth a little way past Ivy.

Eventually, from the other direction, Louie and Anthony came along. They didn't throw anything right away because my beady eyes were on them all the way. They ambled by me and crossed and kept moving, scooping up some slushy snow but waiting for me to turn my back. When they'd just about reached the alley, I turned my back, counted to three, and stepped outside the line of fire.

Splat-splat. Two missiles spattered my heels.

Meanwhile Russo popped out of the alley and fired two ice balls he'd stored back there the night before. The first one missed them both, but the second caught the back of Louie's head like rock on rock. Louie wobbled and turned as Russo jumped back. Then Louie and Anthony ran up the alley, but Russo gave them the slip. I don't think they ever caught on that I had anything to do with it.

It was a while before we discovered they'd got a good look at Russo. If he'd ducked back in that alley a split second sooner, things might have turned out better. And Russo got cocky after that. I had to beg him not to stand on my corner the next afternoon, in case they came back and recognized him.

"They won't" he said. "Anyways, let 'em. Don't nobody push me arahn."

Maybe staying down in the basement so much had worn down his nerves, but he almost seemed to be asking for something bad to happen. Two days later after school he'd gone on home when Louie and Anthony returned with three other guys, including Jimmy.

They asked if I'd seen a kid that looked like Russo, but after that they ignored me completely. Jimmy and another guy hung out on my corner smoking while the rest fanned out around the block. Then they all came back, having found nothing, and all of them vanished. I called Russo that night to warn him and get him to go home some other way than my way for a while. Next morning Arthur came back to school and I turned in my belt.

The funny thing is Jimmy didn't seem to know that Arnold had gone out with Veronica Hilly. He'd taken her on the streetcar out to Kennywood Park just to play a round of goofy golf. According to her, it was none of Jimmy's business because they'd broken up over Christmas, though he gave her a lift now and then. Then all that passed, and life went back to normal, though we kept on watching our backs.

I never meant to let Russo in too much on what was going on with Nikki—not that there was much to tell. But one afternoon, I pulled some cocoons from a briar hedge and took them home and called to ask her if she wanted them. She wasn't home from school yet but her mother said, when she did get home, they might come by for a look. Not long after that, Russo showed up to say hi after hanging out a while across the street with Mr. Marjavi. He and he had been looking over the fat book of rules you had to learn to pass the writing test to get your license. Two minutes after he came in, there was Nikki to see the cocoons. They were on their way to the grocery, and her mom was waiting in the car.

"That was her?" Russo asked me in private when she was gone. "Still got baby dimples."

"Never mind," I said. "There's nothing going on."

"Still, why not fool around a little?"

"With a sixth grade girl?" I said.

"You're still moping over Hatcheck," he said, meaning Margaret. "It's written all over you."

"No, I'm not. And what about you? You still call Patty." Mom had just got another call from Mrs. Colby, asking to ask me to help them stop him from bugging her once and for all.

"Forget that," he said. "So what are you waiting for? You like her?"

"Cut it out," I said.

Next afternoon I went by his place to get back a wrench I'd lent him last fall, and the two of us went up to Sherry's. He was in a rotten mood over all the facts about driving and parts of the driver's handbook he could barely read—which turned out to be almost all. As soon as we let ourselves in, he took one of her cigarettes out of the dish.

"You're gonna smoke?" I said.

"Why not?" He lit up, pocketed another, and took down the garbage. I stayed behind to use the bathroom. Sherry's stockings and underwear were draped around the shower. There were weird kinds of tweezers and other metal tools by the sink, and the bathroom smelled like perfume.

Russo came back up and snapped, "Come outta there!"

I don't think Russo and me ever talked about things like sex again. He still knew things I didn't know, and whatever he didn't know already, he was learning faster than me. But I no longer wanted to ask. A couple nights later, when I called about something else, Bunny said he wasn't home yet, so I asked for him to call me back. By the time he did, I was in bed, and Mom picked up downstairs.

"It's okay, Mom!" I shouted, and ran to their bedroom line.

He told me he'd been at a filling station over on Aiken that stayed open late, helping the night attendant, Stan. Stan went to Pitt all day and studied at night while he was supposedly there to pump gas. Not many wanted gasoline in February at that time of night. Stan let Russo work the pumps and paid him something under the table. It wasn't much, but it beat sitting home in the basement.

"This guy came in tonight and said he lost his keys," Russo told me over the phone. "He's parked down the block. So we lock up the station a minute and go over there and Stan helps him jimmy the window and open the door. Then Stan crawls in and hot-wires the motor, under the dash, so the guy goes on his merry way."

Something didn't sound right. I'd heard about "hot wiring" a car, but I thought it was something illegal.

"Isn't that how cars get stolen?" I asked.

"Naw, it's just how you start a car without the key," he said. "You get down under the dash. There's wires up in there you can take apart and twist together, so then you just press the starter and it starts without the key."

"Like I said," I said.

"Look, we was helping him start his own car."

"How do you know it was his car," I said, "if he didn't have the key?"

"It was his car, okay?" he said. "You think we're stupid? Stan's halfway through college! The point is, I'm learnin' somethin', okay? Anyways, me and Veronica's goin' aht to the goofy golf again sometime. You wanna bring that girl?"

"No," I said. (I decided not to point out there how Russo had started catching bits of Pittsburghese.) "You don't sound very excited yourself."

"Oh, Veron's a good kid and all. . . ."

"But what? She gone back to Jimmy?"

"Not officially. And what do I care? I got other things to think abaht."

"Like what?"

"I'll tell you sometime."

A few days later when Russo was absent, I was coming out of school and Veronica called me over and said, "Tell Russo Jimmy's lookin' for him." That's all she said and walked away.

I went home and tried to call. Nobody answered. I tried again before supper. Still no answer, I guessed Bunny hadn't got home yet and maybe Russo was already working, or else he was down in the basement.

Either way, I wasn't too worried. If he was at the filling station, Stan would be there, and one of them could call the cops if something looked like trouble. If he was home in the basement, that was fine, I could warn him first thing tomorrow at school. A couple hours went by. I began to get nervous again. I decided to tell my parents I'd left something at Bing's or someone else's and I had to go out and get it.

It was after nine by now. The streets were arctic and empty. When I jogged, the pavement slapped my feet. I went all the way to the gas station first, but Russo wasn't there. Back at Russo's, Herbie's car was out front, and the TV flickered inside. That was probably Bunny and Herbie, so I went down the steps by the garbage cans to peek in the cellar window. But everything in there was dark. Was he upstairs with them watching TV? In that case, everything was fine. Or was he lying dead out somewhere? So rather than go on freezing to death, I rang the bell, waited, and rang again. Eventually, Bunny appeared at the door in dumpy slippers and an ugly quilted robe.

"Sorry to bother you, Arnold around?" I asked.

"No, he is not."

"I need to tell him something."

"Did you check the basement?"

"It's dark."

"So he's probably out."

I said sorry again and she went back up. So why was I running around on a freezing night like this? My toes and ankles were numb. I stepped into the street to look at the windows in Sherry's apartment higher up. A dim light sifted out through her curtains. I don't know why but I had the creepy feeling Arnold was up there. But what business of mine was that? I was glad he was probably safe.

I never would have mentioned this to anyone except next day at school he asked me, "What was you doin' last night, barging in on my sister?"

"Looking for you," I said.

"Well, ringin' her bell at ten at night don't score no points with Bunny."

"I wasn't scoring points," I said. "It's just what Veronica said about Jimmy being after you."

"Forget those jerks," he replied. "I see those punks all the time. Heck, they gassed up at the station Sunday night. I told Stanley who they were and he went out and gassed them up himself. All they could do was look at me safe inside. As for last night, whenever you see Herbie's car, just check the basement. I was down there workin' on that stupid driver test."

In the dark? I almost said. Instead I said, "Oh? How's that coming?"

"So-so."

"Not like reading a novel?"

He didn't answer that. He must have known I knew he'd never read one, more than the cover. He could limp through a few words here and there, like a classified ad under *Musical Instruments* if someone like me or his sister had already showed him how to spell *accordion*. He could copy a telephone number and, if he was lucky, get it halfway right. He could get the druggist to read out the address where some pre-scription had to go. He wasn't all that great at street signs but he remembered the names of streets. His memory was good for things like that. He just wasn't

135

good at reading sentences like they wrote in the driver's manual. Especially not in total darkness.

10

I wasn't hanging around up at Nikki's, but once in a while I'd hunt up more cocoons to drop off now and then. The sledding was over and the pond ice never did get hard, so there wasn't much chance I'd run across Wesley or Margaret whenever I trotted up Chatham.

If Nikki was home, I'd also say hi and ask what was up, and maybe drop in for a while. I'd ask how things were going in school; she liked to talk about that. One day I remembered to tell her how Dad's ship, the *Missouri*, hadn't been just a giant gunboat. It was also where the generals from both sides had met to sign the papers that finally ended the war with Japan. She liked that, too. I also did something I'd learned from Russo. Every so often I'd say something like, "Let's think about where we are right now," or "What are you thinking?" Most times she'd answer, but always she'd smile.

One night the Greenbaums took me and my sister to see the Tamburitzans. They were college students at Duquesne who made music and danced like Eastern European peasants. Two guys did that Russian dance where you make windmills out of your legs and then squat down and shoot them out in front of you, one at a time so fast you look like you're bouncing on air. They took me because the accordion player turned out to be their star musician, next to the violin. And what did he play but "Minka, Minka"! When he did, Nikki turned a look on me like she could eat me up.

The Greenbaums did some Japanese hobbies like folding colored squares of paper. Nikki's mother showed me a story they had about a thousand paper cranes. Not only could the whole family fold cranes (even Tommy almost) but Sumi could start out folding a crane and end up making a shrimp or a dog or cicada.

"The funny thing about locusts," I said to them later, thinking aloud, "is how their shell is maybe a sort of cocoon, only not one where they can just hang out all winter. Instead, they have to walk around inside it."

Sumi Greenbaum wanted to write that down. Meanwhile, Nikki said things I might have written down myself. She had questions that didn't occur to other sixth or even eighth grade kids, like why did the bark of a sycamore tree come off like jigsaw puzzle pieces? Or why did countries fight?

Now when Nikki walked me out their driveway, she'd say "See you," like she really hoped she would. And I'd say "See you," too. But on the way home I'd think about Margaret and then feel mad.

One day by the pond Nikki gave me a kiss, and that's how things got started. The rest of those things I'm not gonna say. I don't mind spilling it about Margaret, but things between Nikki and me, well, we figured they were no one's business but our own.

Meanwhile, everyone in Liberty eighth was dying at how slow the days went by. It was still only middle of

March —three more months from graduation! Mrs. Heiler yelled about how we wouldn't feel so high and mighty in September when we started Peabody High and found ourselves in trash barrels rolling down stairs. She also said how hard she prayed she wouldn't be stuck with any of us again next year. She named no names, but she had to mean Russo and several others she never called on to read or diagram a sentence. I'm not sure how he was doing in arithmetic. Maybe Mr. Brooks was letting him off easy. All I knew was that Russo was still getting Mr. Marjavi to help him read the driver's handbook. He'd never pass that test by himself.

One morning when Russo didn't show up, I thought he was cutting again, which surprised me because he had to more desperate than anyone else to pass. That afternoon, Miss Giltenbooth came in and whispered to Mrs. Heiler. Mrs. Heiler waggled a finger at me to send me out in the hall where Miss Giltenbooth told me his sister had telephoned school. Bunny wanted them to let me out so I could go over to her house and talk with her about something. It was only two o'clock, but Miss Giltenbooth said I should go. She'd already called my house and had got my mom's okay. The whole thing was strange, but I went.

When I got there, Bunny sat me down in the kitchen and told me, "Someone beat up Naldy."

She said he was coming home from work last night when a gang had jumped him. He'd run up an alley and climbed a garage where five of them had cornered him. His arm was broken. Some ribs were banged and he had bruises everywhere. We had to take two streetcars to the hospital, in a neighborhood I'd never been.

"He won't tell me who done it or why," she said. "He says no reason. Well, I know my brother, Marty. The reason he won't say who is because he wants to get them back. But you're his friend. He'll tell you who, and when he tells you, you'll tell me, and then I'm callin' the cops."

I nodded like I'd heard, but I didn't actually tell her if I went along with that. I already knew more or less who it was, but if Russo wasn't going to tell, I didn't want to go against him.

The nun at the front desk wore a white starched hat so big she could have sailed the Santa Maria. When she asked how old I was, Bunny cut in and said, "Fifteen," and the nun made a face but let us through.

Russo's room had three empty beds. They'd cranked his up for sitting. His face was bandaged in spots, and a tube ran out of his nose. His left arm wore a plaster cast. His right eye was black. Part of his chest was also bandaged, which made part of his nightshirt bulge. Bunny asked how he was feeling and told him she'd make sure the nurses took good care of him. I'd never seen her so prickly sweet.

He said, "When they lettin' me ahk?" (The tube made him honk.)

"I have no idea," she said, "and don't ask me what this is costin'. You just forget about the money. You're stayin' in here as long as you need to. And that's why you're gonna tell me who did this—so they can pay!"

"I'm payin'," Russo muttered.

"How? By takin' out the trash?" She grabbed his water pitcher and went out to fill it.

I sat by the bed, couldn't think what to say, and for

once he couldn't either, except that talking hurt.

A nurse came in and said, "How's the hero of Guadalcanal?" She stuck a thermometer in his mouth, went out, came back, and read it.

"Am I gekkin' ahk tonike?" he honked.

Bunny came back and pulled me aside to hear if I'd learned any secrets. She had to step out for a bite and a smoke and asked me to stick around and pump him for what he knew. I went to the payphone down the hall, called home to let them know I might stay until seven when visiting hours were over. Then Dad could pick me up.

"Ain'k I pretty?" Russo said when I came back.

"Look," I said, "I know it's my fault."

"Uh-uh, no way," he replied.

"No," I said. "I mean, it was all between me and that bozo Louie and his yo-yo friend. Unless you think Veronica told Jimmy about you were taking her out?"

"She had nothin' da do with ik," he said. After a silence he added, "I called Pak." He turned his head, and when he turned it back I saw a long tear on his cheek.

"You know my trouble?" he said. "I'm dumb."

"You're not dumb," I said.

"I'm dumb. My ribs hurk. My arm hurks. My face hurks. Bunny don' deserve this."

We started wondering how much the cast and the bandages cost and what the doctors got paid, for whatever they'd done to fix his nose. Russo said just climbing into a hospital bed could cost you seventy dollars a night.

"I'll pay her back," he said.

"You going to tell her who did it?" I asked.

"Why?" he said. "She won' get nothin' outta them. Heck, half their dads are cops and firemen. Plus, I did half of this damage myself by jumpin' off the roof."

"They were chasing you," I pointed out. "Look, why not tell?"

"No reason."

Bunny knew him well.

Supper came. I ate the Jell-O.

"Wanna sleep over?" he honked. "I'll only charge you kwenny-five."

Sherry came back picking her teeth and settled on one of the empty beds. "You need more company," she said.

It was only quarter to seven. I decided to wait outside, and Russo didn't stop me. Ten minutes later, Sherry came out and stood nearby where the trolley stopped.

She lit a cigarette and looked at me and said, "Never mind, I'll find out soon enough."

Then Dad pulled up and got me off the hook. But we ended up driving her home.

I felt bad that night. Any way I looked at it, I thought I deserved to get beat up more than Russo. I mean, you couldn't go beating people up for iceballs, not when you threw first. Why it all came down on him, I couldn't understand. But then, I'd got my wish: I'd used to be the goat and now the goat was Russo.

But when he came back to school, the whole class wanted to sign his cast. The bandages were off his face, but his nose was dented. He looked like Marlon Brando looked at the end of "On the Waterfront" after getting beat up by the goons. Russo said he'd fallen off his bike, and only Veronica and me knew different.

Well, you know Russo, or should by now. He had to get Jimmy back, but I didn't expect him to try so soon. It was only the end of March, and his left arm was still in the cast. Veronica had come to school that day with an engagement ring, but it wasn't from Jimmy. It was from some guy who'd just got out of the Airborne.

That evening Russo called me, angry. A short while before, Jimmy and the rest of those monkeys had pulled right into the station while Russo was one-handedly gassing someone else's car. He didn't see the Stoodie until its brights were in his face.

"Arnold! Hey! C'mere!" said Jimmy, rolling down the window.

Russo couldn't bring himself to be smart and call on Stan for help right away or beat it back to the office. He walked around and asked what Jimmy wanted.

"Fill 'er up," said Jimmy.

While Russo pumped the gas, Jimmy got out and asked him where he'd got the cast. Russo said nothing. He just shut up and filled the tank and told Jimmy what he owed.

"You alone?" said Jimmy.

In fact Stan was right inside, but you can guess what Russo said:

"Jus' me."

Jimmy gave him a dollar. Russo handed it back and said, "This ain't four bucks, twenty-one cents."

Jimmy waved his you-know-what finger, got back in, and burned rubber back to the street. Russo yelled and went inside and told Stan how he'd been stiffed, which made him also finally tell Stan the truth of how he'd broken his arm. The problem was, since Russo was being paid under the table, Stan couldn't just call the police.

"Never mind," Russo concluded. "I got it worked aht better than Jimmy."

"What do you mean?" I said.

"Just don't be tied up Saturday night."

"Why not?"

"Because that's March thirty-first."

"So?"

"Think! What month comes after March?"

"April. So?" Sunday was April Fool's.

"Be over my place around dark," he said. "And bring a flashlight. And gloves."

"Why?"

"Just bring 'em. And stop lookin' nervous. It's no big deal. You'll only be scoutin'."

"For what?"

All else he would say was either I showed up or not.

It's strange. Somehow, the person I most wanted to talk about this with was Mrs. Greenbaum or maybe even Nikki. I don't know what they would have said, but talking about it might have helped. But I remembered how palling around with Russo had messed me up with the Hatchecks and I didn't want that to happen again if I told the Greenbaums about him, too. Plus, then they might know too much about what I was really like. As it was, I didn't talk to anyone, but Mom looked at me funny when I went out that Saturday night. She knew the night before April Fool's was when even some nice boys roamed around soaping the windows on cars, turning over people's trash and tossing toilet paper around over trees and electrical wires. She didn't think that I would do that, and it ran against her principles to treat me like I would. So all she could do was make me take an umbrella, since the weatherman said rain. But it didn't feel like rain to me, so I left the umbrella at Russo's and the two of us headed out.

"Where to?" I asked.

"Don't worry," he said. "You're only the lookout."

"What are you going to do?"

"Don't worry."

"Famous last words," I said.

A few streets later we stopped. He pointed up the block and said, "That's it. That's Jimmy's house."

"How do you know?"

"Veronica told me. And there's his car."

"What?" I stared and saw he was right. Up the block was the car that looked more like a fighter than any car that had ever been, or ever would be made: my beautiful Stoodie, its aero-blue an ivory-white in the pale-night, drizzly street. It wasn't parked right outside Jimmy's, but a house or two further down.

"What are we going to do?" I said.

"Take it."

"Get aht 'a here," I said.

"I knew you'd be chicken."

"I'm not chicken. I'm just not stupid! What happens when they catch us?"

"Who?"

"The police."

"I gotta do it," he said.

"Anyways, who's going to drive it? You don't even have a learner's permit."

"I know how to drive."

"With one arm? And without any keys?"

"For one thing, it ain't locked" he said. "The driver-side vent has a broken latch. You can reach in around and pull the handle inside the door."

"Yeah, but what about starting it?"

Russo reached his good arm into his jacket. He pulled out some pliers and a couple other tools and said, "Where's the flashlight?"

I gave him the flashlight saying, "Take it. From here on, count me out."

He looked at me, and I shrank. I mean, there he was with the broken arm he'd got on account of me, the cast poking out the sleeve of his dad's old coat from the merchant marine. He'd got that cast and the dent in his nose because of something he'd done for me. I was the one kid in the universe he had the right to ask.

"Okay," he said. "Go home."

"It's crazy."

"Go home. Go on. But first stand over there and tell me if anyone comes while I'm workin' under the dash. Then go on home and suit yourself."

"Okay," I said, "but that's it."

The car was in a great spot, a few doors up and facing away. In every nearby house, the lights were off, at least in the rooms downstairs. Only one first-floor window was lit and inside that one, behind a thin curtain, sat an old lady, head bent, stitching in a pool of light.

"She'll see you," I told him.

He shrugged. "She's pro'lly blind. And what she care?"

From across the street I watched. I could see Jimmy's dark front porch. I could see the driver's side of the Stoodie and, just over its roof and across the sidewalk, the hunched old lady sewing away. Meanwhile Russo sidled up to the car. He folded out the driver-side vent and tried to stick his good right arm inside to reach the inside handle on the door, but he couldn't because using his right arm made him need to twist around too much.

This is stupid! I kept thinking. *We'll both end up in Western Penitentiary.*

He looked across at me and for a moment I thought he was going to ask me to come back over and reach in with my own left arm. Then he looked at the old lady in her window. She had spectacles that dangled out at the point of her nose. Then Russo looked back at the vent. He put his right arm back inside and twisted in a different direction, got hold of something and started to bob up and down at the knees.

What's he doing? I wanted to know. Up and down, up and down he bobbed half a dozen times. Then he stopped, withdrew his arm, and I could see what he'd done. He'd rolled down the window. Now he reached in through the open window and stepped back as the driver-side door swung open. Then he squatted by the open seat and slid in under the steering wheel and all.

147

So there he was, hind legs stuck out in the glow of the streetlight, easy to see for anyone on my side of the street. That's how he lay there, twisting around and doing stuff forever under the dash. *Forever and ever*, like the teachers reading ten verses of the Bible to us every day and the ones they like best are, *Yea, though I walk through the valley of the shadow of death I shall fear no evil for I shall dwell in the house of the Lord forever and ever*, which also reminded me again of jail. That's how long it seemed to me, standing there, on legs as weak as spaghetti.

Finally he shimmied out and climbed into the seat, waving me over and shutting his door. The old lady lifted her nose at the sound.

"C'mon!" Russo whispered as loud as he could.

The old lady stood up and turned to the window, though how much she could see through her Irish curtain I will never know. I hurried across and around to the passenger side, my face turned away from her view.

"Get in!" he said, releasing my door. "You're gatherin' a crahd aht there!"

That was true. Now I was the only one of us two that anyone could see who he was, so I was the one they'd tell the police they'd seen stealing Jimmy's car; so I climbed in, too, and closed the door (more loudly than I meant). By now the old lady had drawn back the curtain and was holding the phone to her face. Then the curtain dropped back and I knew she was dialing.

Meanwhile, Russo had pressed some button or flicked some switch because suddenly the motor was on and the Stoodie trembled like it had swallowed something hard to digest.

"She's callin'!" I said, meaning the lady.

"Callin' for the open road!" said Russo, meaning the car. "Here goes nothin'."

He turned the wheel all the way left as fast as he could with one good arm, shifted the stick, and gave her gas.

Bonk! We lurched and the engine went dead.

"What's wrong?" I said.

"I dunno." He looked around. "Emergency brake," he concluded, rammed it in, and tried the starter again. We swung out into the street and nearly ploughed into a car parked on the other side before Russo wrestled us right.

"Great start!" I said.

"You bet!"

But sure enough, we were rollin'.

"Stop sign!" I yelled near the corner.

"I see it! Shut up while I drive!"

I said no more, and after that he really did seem to know how to drive, though later he said we were lucky the Stoodie had automatic transmission. We would have had loads of fun—him with his broken arm, driving with manual gears.

A pair of headlights came at us and honked, and Russo veered out of their way, swearing at the crazy driver. After that, he stayed more on our side of the street. A couple blocks later, another car passed and honked, and the driver yelled, "Idiot! Lights!"

Russo reached around on his left until he found something that turned the headlights on. We were eight or ten blocks from where we'd started when he finally pulled in and stopped along the curb. The first thing he did was put on gloves to wipe his fingerprints off the wheel.

149

"Okay, I've had enough," I said, my feet on the metal coverings that Russo had removed from under the dash.

"Relax. What's your hurry?"

"Arnold!"

"Listen, wha' cha hear?"

"The motor."

"Six cylinders, baby. What else?"

"Look, we're not really stealing his car?"

"Nah. Just drive around a while and leave it somewhere hard to find."

"Let's leave it here," I said.

He wasn't listening. He was eyeing Jimmy's lucky fuzzy dice, which dangled over the dash.

"That's a safety hazard: it blocks the view," he declared. "It's in the book." He snapped them off their strings and tossed under my feet.

"I like this car," he said. "If it was mine, next thing I'd do is put one of those suicide knobs here on the wheel so I could spin it easier."

I said, "Look, you're not gonna steal it, are you? Because if you are, you're crazy."

"*'That's me, Major.'*"

"Russo, you are!"

"Okay, okay." He sat a minute, reached across me to the glove compartment, found a pack of Camels and took one out.

I said. "I'm not sitting here waiting for the cops while you kill yourself from cancer."

"Listen," he said. He looked up at the patter of rain on the roof.

"It's barely raining," I said. "Let's go."

I got out, turned up my collar and walked. Behind

me sat the Stoodie like a friendly, wide-eyed carnivore, headlights on and running, as Russo invented his next big move. I was just to the corner when there came Pollock, Crocker, Bing, and Snyder up the side street.

"Hey, Marteeny, April Fools!" said Pollock, doing a windshield with a bar of soap.

"Hey, Marty, heard the news?" said Crocker, waving his own Ivory bar. "Ralph Colby's taking Margaret to his senior prom."

"Oh yeah?" I said.

"Yeah," said Teddy. "Big surprise." He looked around and asked, "Where's the yo-yo?"

"Who?"

"Russo. Don't tell us you left him at home?"

"How would I know?" I said.

"Well, you're always together."

"So, Marteeny," said Wesley. "How's your Oriental kewpie?"

I don't know how long I stood there saying nothing but looking daggers first at Wesley and then at them all. Long enough for them to look at me funny, say more things I didn't care for, and head away without me. I returned to the Stoodie and climbed back in. Russo sat there lighting Jimmy's Camel on the car's electric lighter.

"What are you doin' here?" he asked.

And I said, "What are you?"

"Just thinkin'," he said.

We wove our way up to Fifth and followed it east to Washington Boulevard, the same long, potholed road we'd pedaled down last fall on bikes. Only this time, there I was riding with Russo in that 1950 bullet-nosed wonder, the car of my dreams, to that final dogfight in the sky.

The final stoplight blinked yellow. We passed empty welding yards and truck lots and under the arch of Larimer Avenue Bridge. Russo had turned on the heat. I took off my gloves and was fiddling with the radio, tuning in on Porky Chadwick until Russo said to shut him off. The moment was too pure for jive. I stretched my legs and kicked away the dice and tools and metal covers that Russo had stripped from under the dash. I pocketed one of my gloves but couldn't find the other.

"Can't find my other glove," I said. Russo turned on the cabin light, which was way at the back, just front of the wide back window, and didn't cast much light up front. The boulevard smoothed and straightened toward the river. On the left we passed the fire department's baby-dropping tower.

"Ever think of bein' one of them?" asked Russo.

"I used to," I admitted. "I used to have a Texaco Fire Chief's hat, and a fire truck when I was six. And firehat lollipops, too."

"I could do that," he said. He started singing the second part of that song called "Lazy Mary":

> *Lazy Mary, you smoke in bed,*
> *There's only one man you should marry.*
> *My advice to you would be....*

The song went on, recommending that lazy Mary find herself a fireman for a husband in case she set the sheets of fire; but Russo shut up as we passed the barracks of the Pennsylvania State Police. Two troopers with rain covers over their Smokey-Bear hats were standing out by one of the cars.

"Uh-oh," he said, a quarter mile later. "Look back and see if it's them."

I looked. There was some sort of car a ways behind but probably gaining.

"Dunno," I said. I don't see a light on top."

"They wouldn't turn that on yet, not while they're sneakin' up."

"Yep, I think it's them," I said a moment later. "How fast are you going?"

"Lemme see." Then he sped up, saying the idea was to not go so slow that you looked like you were up to something.

"Look front!" he said. "Don't let them see you starin' aht the back."

His face was shiny with sweat.

"There it is," he said.

We stared ahead at the yellow arrows where the boulevard ended at River Road. "Look back and watch their blinkers. Whichever way they mean to turn, we'll turn the other way."

That didn't work because the troopers were behind us, and they didn't need to blink until we did. So, when we came to the end of the boulevard, Russo swung us right without blinking or stopping but slow enough so the tires eeked but didn't scream. I looked back to see which way they'd turn. It looked like they'd stopped at the junction and were making up their minds.

Now rising on our right was the cliff at Brilliant Cutoff. On the left, a chain-link fence cut us off from some woods that ran down toward the banks of Allegheny River. Russo spotted an opening ahead in the fence. He slowed us down a tad and fishtailed left. As we passing through a gate, out of the dark a sign reared up that looked to me like *BRILLIANT CUTOFF LUNCH*. I wondered if we were heading down to some riverside joint where speedboat people hung out—maybe even the Thunderbird Lodge.

We wove down a broad muddy track.

"What the heck?!" said Russo.

By the time those words were out we were sliding down a narrow, concrete ramp.

Russo pressed the brake but had to let up as the car began to twist.

"Stop!" I shouted.

We were skidding slowly, slightly sideways, like the concrete was covered with grease. Algae slime is what it turned out to be. He managed to straighten us out, and as he did, our headlights raked the river fifteen yards ahead. He tried to throw her into reverse, but the engine barked and stalled. Still nothing stopped our slide.

"Out!" he ordered.

He twisted his good right arm around and somehow opened the driver side door. I opened mine and tumbled out onto the edge of the ramp, then off it onto some good-sized rocks. By the time I was right-side-up again, the Stoodie had slid to a stop below, its nose about touching the water. It looked like it wanted a drink.

"Russo? Russo?"

"Yo!" he called. "You okay?"

"Are you?"

I climbed back onto the ramp, slipped on the slime, and slid down ten feet further where I passed underneath the back bumper until my elbows planted on something. I might have slid all the way under the Stoodie and into the river, if I hadn't been snagged by the license plate of the Keystone State.

Russo got up from the stones on the other side, worked his way down, and helped me crabwalk off the ramp. We hung onto each other, staring at what we'd done and wondering what to do. The headlights and taillights were all still on. The doors hung open on either side.

"Could we pull it back?" I said.

"We could try," he said, not sounding hopeful. "Get around the other side again, and grab on wherever you can."

There was no footing on the ramp, but maybe if I wedged my feet in the rocks...? Well, it was stupid—no way the two of us were going to pull that Stoodie back, but we had to give it a shot. I wormed across, wedged my feet, and got set up at my end of the bumper.

"Ready?" he said.

"Ready."

"On three. One,... two,...."

We groaned and pulled. Instead of coming our way, the Stoodie launched into more forward progress.

"It's goin'!" he yelled, and I let go.

Now the grill was underwater. The engine spat and hissed. Steam poured out in a cloud and something up front went *Crack!* Russo said later it must have been the engine block splitting in two. Now the car lights were dead, and all that glittered were streetlamps in Aspinwall, far off on the other side. The river poured into the Stoodie.

We didn't stick around. We scrambled up the sides of the ramp and up that muddy road. We'd passed the sign near the gate (what it really said was *BRILLIANT*

CUTOFF LAUNCH) and were scrambling out to River Road when a pair of headlights drove us back into hiding. We dove behind the sign in time to dodge a pickup truck turning in where we were. A guy hung out the passenger window saying, "I swear I seen it, man!" The driver must have known this place because he'd slowed way down and stopped before they got close to the ramp. Three guys piled out and, as they picked their way down toward the water, we ran out the way we'd come. Again we ducked in the bushes as a trooper car passed with its siren on.

We ran. From the boulevard, we climbed the woody hill that took us up into Highland Park. By then the rain had let up. Around half-past midnight, back in Russo's basement, we cleaned up as well as we could. His cast was ruined. He might have left chunks of it all over Jimmy's front seat. Also, his bracelet was missing, along with my other glove. The good thing was that all the bracelet said was *ARNOLD* and lots of people had that name. The bad thing was the glove was the one that Mom had sewn the label in.

But I was too beat to care about that. I was punchy, giddy-tired as we stripped and sloshed our things in a washtub with laundry soap to cut the slime. Russo snuck upstairs for something to put on while the furnace dried my things. I decided against calling home so late. My parents might be worried; on the other hand, they might have gone to bed. In that case, I'd rather sneak in and hope I wouldn't wake them up.

"Pretty good night," said Russo.

"Great." And I meant it. "Except I lost my glove."

"Then pray to St. Anthony."

"Who's he?"

"He helps you find things when they're lost. All you gotta say is, 'Tony, Tony, look arahn'; somethin's lost and must be fahnd'.'"

St. Jude, he said, was also good for that and other things. St. Jude was the saint of lost causes. You prayed to him when things were hopeless. And I was almost sure by then we'd never get away with it. Plus, Russo's arm was aching. He'd messed up the bone, and he'd find out later it meant he'd have to have a new cast made and wear it another two months. My things weren't drying, so I went home in some of Russo's clothes. The last thing I did before I left was make him swear that what we'd done that night did settle his score with Jimmy.

"Heck," he said, "we was just gettin' started." Then he grabbed me, saying, "Man, the things you get me into, and you know I've done some crazy things."

"That's right, you do," I said.

"But I never would've done it if you hadn't been with me all the way."

"Sure," I said. "Only next time wait until you got your driver's license."

"I drove okay!" he protested. "And how am I supposed to get the license when I can't read the goddamn book? Hey, you gonna make it home all right?"

I did, but Mom was still up. She asked me if I'd been out soaping windows at one in the morning and I shrugged like maybe I had. That's what made her angry.

"Very nice," she said. "Well, it serves you right—ruining a brand new coat and losing a new leather glove!"

I didn't tell her which.

157

It took about six weeks for the *shinto* (as Dad said once) to hit the fan. Meanwhile the cocoons were starting to open. She called me when the first one popped in April, then two in the first week of May. Each time, she'd open the jar and let it fly away.

That's around the time I made another mistake that I regret much more than I regret the car. Nikki was having a party, and Pammy and I were invited. But Pammy didn't want me there, and I used that as my excuse. I had no idea what kind of party it was going to be, but with mostly sixth graders I knew it wouldn't be for me, so I didn't go. I didn't realize what I'd done until I went up Saturday morning to look at the jars and realized Nikki's disappointment. I asked her how the party went, and all she said was, "Fine." I offered to stick around a little, but she had other things to do. Any dummy knew I'd hurt her feelings.

In the middle of May, the Russians put up Sputnik 3 without any hitches, but the next day Mom blew up. The police had come by asking questions. It turns out the Stoodie had gone about ten feet under water and they'd had to tow it out. Then someone had found Russo's bracelet, snagged under the seat. They tracked him down through the picture of Patty. Once they did, between the bracelet and plaster scraps inside the car, it wasn't hard to pin the crime on Russo. How they got me as well, I wasn't sure. It could have been the glove; or maybe Wesley or Crocker had ratted after seeing me on the night of April Fool's, or else maybe Patty or Margaret had told the juvenile detectives things about Russo and me.

"Marty, this is crime," said my mother. "I'm very, very ashamed," she said. "And don't ever lie to me again. Ever," she said.

"I never lied," I said. "You were the one that said I'd been out soaping windows. I never said I was."

"Don't argue! What's come over you? You don't say anything anymore. We try to do somewhere nice, and you grouch and say you have to do something with Arnold Russo."

"Sorry."

"Sorry will not do, young man. Are you still upset about Margaret?"

"What are you talking about?"

"You know what you've done is the kind of thing that can send a boy your age...."

"I know that."

"How could you let yourself be used by someone like Arnold? Not only a boy with no self-control, but very, very mixed up. A very sad young man."

"I know. He's weird."

"No child should grow up like that. I almost think they should go ahead and.... Maybe that would straighten him out. You know where he is now, don't you?"

"No."

"He's halfway to downtown, locked up at Juvenile Hall."

"Mom, you were the one who told me to be friends with him."

159

"Not meaning to let him turn you into...!"

"Well, anyways," I said, "I'm sorry."

"There's *anyways* again! You could be down there, too. But you know why not?"

"Why."

"Because of your parents. With parents like us, the authorities know, whatever you did, it wasn't you that did it."

"Look, you can lay off Russo," I said.

"Do not say *look* when there's nothing to—"

"Mom! You don't know how me and Russo—"

"*Me and Russo*?! *Russo and I*!" Don't ever say these things again!"

I turned away.

"Stop," she ordered. "And put your jacket back on."

"Why?"

"Because we're going to the Greenbaums."

"Fer what?"

She glared—but let it pass and said, "Because we need some advice, and Sumi told us how Fred's sister is a lawyer on the—"

"You can't tell the Greenbaums," I said.

"Don't interrupt me. We most certainly can. We're only waiting for your father."

"May I have permission to go upstairs until he comes?"

"And do what?"

"And practice for my lesson tonight with Mr. Marjavi."

"You're not having any lesson."

"Why?"

"Because Mr. Marjavi had a heart attack this morning."

"And you're blaming that on me?"

"Of course not."

"Is he sick?"

"He's very sick."

"Well, while we wait for Dad, can I go across and see him?"

"He's in the hospital."

That was sad. I thought a little.

"Well," I said, "can you wait here and I'll go up to the Greenbaums' myself and you can meet me there? I promise not to run away."

I could see this was the end of everything with Nikki, and I wanted to go up and tell before they told her what I'd done. Not that there had ever been much hope between us. How could there? It bugged me, thinking as I walked up there, *Why is everyone stuck in their age? We're trapped that way. Look at me and look at Russo, or look at a girl* like *Veronica Hilly. Look at our parents or Mrs. Heiler. Look at me and Nikki.* How could there be anything, when me and her—*I and she* or *she and I*—were two years apart? What makes even a single year become such a long, long difference? I just wanted to see her again in private before they sent me to reform school.

When I got there Nikki was out kneeling on the lawn. She had one of the jars between her knees. She stopped waiting for me to kneel down beside her to open it and let the little critter go—a small, brown moth that had just emerged from a bean-sized tent. Nothing special, just brown like most of the rest.

"That's the last," she said.

We sat on the lawn and played with the grass. The sun was warm. She was wearing the butterfly pin.

"We're leaving," she said.

"What?"

"In June. Papa's boss is moving him to Arizona."

"Why?"

"He says it's a place to sell windows."

I couldn't believe it.

"Phoenix, Arizona," she said. "Like the bird."

"The thunderbird?"

"No, the phoenix, that rises out of the fire."

"Wow."

"I know."

Well, her family was bound to reject me anyway, when they heard what my parents would say. From then on, she and I were toast. They'd chase me off as fast as the Colbys chased off Russo.

"I'm sorry you missed the party," she said.

"Me, too."

"No, you aren't," she said.

"I was!"

She kissed me on the cheek and smiled like a squirrel.

"I'm serious!" I kissed her back on the dimple. We might have gone on, but suddenly my folks were in the drive. We stood up.

"Order in the court," I said.

She said, "I'm not supposed to be there while you're talking with my aunt. They said you'd feel better like that."

"I guess," I said. "Well, no, not really."

I should get back to Mr. Marjavi. It was true he'd had

a heart attack and it wasn't on account of me, though it turns out he knew about what we'd done. Or some of it. He knew what Russo had done. Russo never did name me.

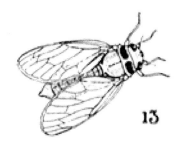

13

So the five-star generals met: my parents, the Green-baum and the lawyer aunt, Marjory Kaplan. About me. Meanwhile, Pam and Nikki were sent to the other end of the house to keep the other Greenbaum children busy and out of hearing.

"Where do we start?" asked the aunt. She'd said she had some way of talking to someone at juvenile court.

"He's not admitting right now that he did it," Mom began. "Or should he?"

"Did what?" asked the aunt. "Drive off with the car?"

"He wasn't driving," said Dad.

"Took a ride with his friend?" the lawyer aunt suggested.

"I did that," I said.

The aunt turned to me and said, "Marty, the way I've heard the story so far, you and the older boy broke into another boy's car. Is that—?"

"It wasn't locked," said Mom.

"It was, we unlocked it," I said. "But the driver-side vent—"

"Hush," said Mom. "Just answer Mrs. Kaplan's questions."

The aunt raised a hand. "Let me speak with Marty a minute. Marty, the way I've heard it, first you and the young man got into the car and drove it a few blocks away. Am I right so far?"

"Right."

"Then you got out, because you'd wanted him to leave it there. You walked down the block and ran into some friends from school, out wandering around on April Fool's eve, and said something to them, and they said something back—"

"I didn't say anything first," I said.

"But they said something to you. Something that made you change your mind and go back to the car."

I nodded.

"What did they say?"

"Something."

"About what?"

"Something else."

"Someone else?"

I nodded.

"Who?"

I shrugged.

"Look," said Mr. Greenbaum, "isn't the point that Marty's been implicated mainly by his connection to the older boy? They were known as friends, but the woman who called the police—could she say for sure it was Marty? So unless this Arnold says it was Marty— and even if he says it was—really, none of this may have been Marty's idea. If Marty steps forward honestly now, don't you think the judge might...?"

I knew it. They wanted me to hang it on Russo and say that I never had any intention of stealing the car in the first place. Meanwhile, I sure as shootin' knew that Russo would never spill the beans on me.

"You want me to rat," I mumbled.

"Speak up, Marty," said Mom.

"You want me to rat on Russo."

They looked at each other.

"Well, no," said Mr. Greenbaum. "See, there's a difference between—"

Mrs. Kaplan held up her hand for quiet and said, "Marty, tell me, what made you get back in the car?"

"You mean why?" I said. By now I was almost willing to tell. But I kept thinking how all of this would eventually get back to Nikki, this business of what my "friends" had called her. She could have taken it, I guess. Who knows, she might have up and socked them in the kisser. But why should she need to do that?

"I guess I was upset," I said.

"About what?"

"Things."

"What things?"

"Just things."

Mrs. Kaplan asked some other questions, expressed her own opinions, and ended by saying all that mattered was the judge. Then she and the Greenbaums left the room so my parents could give me a talking to. After that I didn't feel like riding home with them in the car. I told them to pick up Pamela along the way (she and Nikki hadn't taken the little kids down to the pond), and I'd walk home by myself. I didn't say so, but part of it was I wanted to say goodbye to Nikki now, since this looked like the end of the line.

I gave them a couple minutes to leave, then went outside and came across Mrs. Greenbaum with her garden apron on, kneeling over a bucket of currant plants she'd dug up down at Paradise. I should have mentioned the lot had been sold. The *FOR SALE* signs were already gone and some big machines were already there to bulldoze and dig out a basement for a new apartment building. Sumi was troweling holes for replanting the currants in their yard. On top of the pile of dirt, an inch-long, yellow-white grub lay upside down waving its legs.

"Mrs. Greenbaum?"

"Yes?"

"Um, that thing I said to Reggie last fall, the 'Bombs away. . . .'"

"We understand. You were trying to amuse him. You wanted to make it more fun."

"So, anyway, I'm sorry."

She settled back on her knees. "You know, Marty," she said, "we're glad you've been good friends with Nikki. She appreciates you very much. And I appreciated your getting her to read that story about the thousand paper cranes."

"I did?"

"The first time she opened it and saw how short all the sentences were, she thought it was for someone younger. But then when she saw you read a chapter, she gave it a second chance. Marty, you know we're moving?"

I nodded. "Nikki told me."

"We hadn't expected to leave so soon."

"Me, neither," I said.

It was a big deal around Liberty School that Russo and I'd been arrested. Crocker made bets about us winding up either in Sing-Sing or Lewisburg Prison. Bunny tried to get Stan to go and tell how Jimmy had ripped off Arnold for that seventeen gallons of gas. But Stanley wouldn't go, on account of losing his job if the boss found out he'd been paying Russo under the table. Russo might have done time at Warrendale Youth Detention Camp, except Sherry spoke on his behalf.

My parents paid for the damage, including the engine and ruined seats. They didn't have to pay a lot because the car was eight years old, and the judge said Jimmy could get the parts from a junkyard. They even paid for the wreckage the tow truck made of the back of the Stoodie, hauling it out of the river. I never went to jail, either, and we both got to finish Liberty School.

Russo never stopped wondering why the State Troopers had followed our car—if that's what we'd been seeing behind us. Maybe one of Jimmy's taillights was out before we ever stole the car, or maybe we'd left the cabin light on after I looked for that glove. That's another one of the million things the driver's manual says is illegal. I didn't see Russo the rest of the summer—the judge said we couldn't hang out—and after June his sister moved to the North Side where he went to trade school—for boilermakers I think. As for his accordion, their new place didn't have any basement, so even after his arm was okay his sister made him pawn it.

As for Bing and the rest, I didn't see them much in high school, where the students came from all over. I didn't have many classes with them anymore. In high school Bing was still "the King" in sports and things, but by then I wasn't jealous anymore.

I don't know what more to say about Nikki and me. We got a little carried away the last few weeks before she left. It was like that jazz song by Peggy Lee about how someone gives you fever. But no one made either of us go to confession and there was nothing we'd either regret. I also gave her the thunderbird ring, which she kept. (Mrs. Hatfield had mailed it back). We called it a friendship ring and she said she'd go on wearing it (taped to make it fit) after they moved. Dad said he and I might drive out there some summer, once I was old enough to drive. I think it was memories of Nikki that laid me low my first few years of high school, as far as girls were concerned. But then we lost touch. I remember her writing how blue she was feeling around the time she turned thirteen, and me writing back to let her know it only lasted a year.

As for Mr. Marjavi, I saw him a few times more before he died, but not for lessons. When we saw him at the hospital, he gave us the number of Mr. di Bono, another accordion teacher who'd never stop yelling about my left arm. Mr. M was sorry Russo had stopped taking lessons because, of all his students the past few years, Russo came closest right away to understanding how music was made. With Arnold, Mr. Marjavi had never even needed to mention the thing about arms. Then the Marjavis moved to a tiny apartment that didn't have steps. By that time I was pretty rusty. Still, whenever I sit down to play, I think about the left arm places in my life, and I try to catch up a little with Russo.

A funny thing is that now and then I still see Jimmy's Stoodie: I see half of it, I mean. I see it on Howe Street now and then. Jimmy had fixed the front end mostly, when he noticed stuff wrong with the back end that maybe the tow truck had caused. Around then, he sold it off to a man with a very unusual sense of humor. That guy cut off the whole back half with a blow torch and scrapped it. Then he welded the front half of that 1950 Studebaker onto the back half of a 1950s Willys Jeep station wagon. Try and draw that if you can. You'll never see a weirder car.

Thanks to Joyce Baker who hatched this creature and Tamim Ansary who watches the brood.

Thanks to Robert Evans Snodgrass for art from *Insects, Their Way and Means of Living*, to Billy Rose and Lee David for "Tonight You Belong to Me," and Lou Monte for "Lazy Mary."

CPSIA information can be obtained at www.ICGtesting.com
Printed in the USA
BVOW010542150713

325880BV00005B/40/P

9 780977 708253